ıry Cecil was the pseudonym of Judge Henry Cecil
ın. He was born in Norwood Green Rectory, near
ıdon, England in 1902. He studied at Cambridge
ıre he edited an undergraduate magazine and wrote a
ılights May Week production. Called to the bar in
∠3, he served with the British Army during the Second
ıld War. While in the Middle East with his battalion he
ı d to entertain the troops with a serial story each
ıning. This formed the basis of his first book, *Full Circle*.
ı was appointed a County Court Judge in 1949 and held
ı t position until 1967. The law and the circumstances
ıich surround it were the source of his many novels,
ıys, and short stories. His books are works of great
ı nic genius with unpredictable twists of plot which
ılight the often absurd workings of the English legal
ıstem. He died in 1976.

BY THE SAME AUTHOR
ALL PUBLISHED BY HOUSE OF STRATUS

DAUGHTERS
IN LAW

by

Henry Cecil

HOUSE OF
STRATUS

This edition published in 2000 by House of Stratus, an imprint of Stratus Holdings plc, 24c Old Burlington Street, London, W1X 1RL, UK.

www.houseofstratus.com

Typeset, printed and bound by House of Stratus.

A catalogue record for this book is available from the British Library.

ISBN 1-84232-049-1

Contents

CHAPTER ONE

Down with the Law

Some otherwise mild-mannered people become aggressive or offensive or at least lose some control of themselves when confronted with something or somebody they particularly hate. It is almost like a physical ailment, just as some asthmatics start to lose their breath if there is a cat in the house, even if they don't know it. So, when mention is made of beatniks or psychiatrists or politicians or dramatic critics or whatever his aversion happens to be, the normally gentle, kindly person either withdraws into himself or lets fly.

With Major Claude Buttonstep it was lawyers. But he did have to know they were there. He could not sense their presence. If one of his sons was out with Prunella Coombe, a barrister, or the other with her twin sister, Jane, a solicitor, he would be perfectly happy as long as he did not know it or suspect it. But the idea of either of his boys marrying a lawyer was horrible to him. He was a man with a swift imagination. If you were late for an appointment with him, he had you run over by an omnibus, attended your funeral and, if you were important enough, he had written an additional obituary for you in *The Times* – modestly preceded by 'CB writes' – provided, of course, you weren't a lawyer. So, if he thought that Prunella was out with his elder son Digby at a cinema or that Jane was dancing with his younger son John, he could picture himself staying away from the christening and even refusing to acknowledge his grandchild.

Major Buttonstep had some cause for disliking lawyers. His family in each generation, as far as he could trace them, had become engaged in costly litigation. What the Revenue had not taken from the family estates the lawyers had. Major Buttonstep, instead of being able to enjoy the life of a country gentleman like his predecessors, had been compelled to work for his living. He forgave the Revenue because it was impartial. It taxed everyone. He could not forgive the lawyers. Everyone was a victim of the tax-gatherer, it was the few whose blood the lawyers sucked.

He kicked against work as long as he could, but when he was actually threatened with a summons for rates, there was no alternative. Even work was preferable to being caught up by the law. He paid his rates and joined the Army. And eventually he retired with the rank of major. Fortunately he married a girl with means of her own so that, when he retired, they had sufficient to live on and to bring up their two sons.

They lived happily in the country near London. They were popular and respected in the neighbourhood and the major was even invited to become a Justice of the Peace. He refused with indignation. He would not be contaminated with even that much of the law.

'But we're not lawyers,' his friend remonstrated, 'we have a clerk to tell us what the law is – or rather what he thinks it is. He doesn't always get it right, but that's not our fault. We just deal with the facts, and we want fair-minded chaps like you on the Bench to counteract some of the Socialists we're getting.'

'Never,' said Major Buttonstep. 'A Conservative lawyer is as bad as a Socialist lawyer. He's probably worse. Charges more.'

'But we're not lawyers, Claude,' protested his friend.

'You carry out the law, don't you?' growled the major.

'Well, of course, we have to.'

'Then, as far as I'm concerned, you're lawyers. Upon my word, I believe one of the family was ruined by chaps like you. A case of poaching it was. The fellow bagged a pheasant and it dropped in the road. Now any sensible honest chap would have said that was poaching. The fellow even admitted it when he was caught. But would that do for the lawyers? Oh dear me no. Where actually was it when it was shot? It might have been over the road. If it was over the road, was it on public property? I tell you they argued for two years about whether that road was public property or not, and they argued for another two whether it made any difference. You won't believe this, but it's true. After two years they found the road was public property, and after the other two they found it didn't make any difference. The fellow'd gone to Australia by then. How often have you done that?'

'We've never had a case which lasted more than a week. You can't really mean it took two years.'

'Oh, not just in your court. You don't think the lawyers would be satisfied with that? No wigs and gowns there. Oh, no. Somehow or other they got it to the High Court with three flipping judges looking at fifty flipping books and asking fifty million flipping questions about them. Two counsel on each side – all in flipping wigs and gowns, and another chap, who didn't seem to do anything, sitting below the judges. He had a flipping wig and gown too. Wonder what that cost. I was a boy and saw it all. My father thought it would interest me. Interest me! Here was a fellow caught poaching. Red-handed. Admitted it. And to hear the Lord Chief Justice talking, you'd think it was the Tichborne case all over again.

' "Tell me, Sir Bloomer," I remember him saying, "how do you reconcile the case of Coster and Bursnip with Featherspoon and Idle?" – those weren't the real names, but my memory isn't as good as it was – "how do you reconcile them?" he said. And d'you know, that fellow, Bloomer Wilkins his name was, at least it sounded like that – they'd knighted him for not becoming a judge or something – d'you know, he went on for two days explaining why he *couldn't* reconcile them. And, would you believe it, at the end of the two days the Lord Chief Justice smiled and said: "Well, Sir Bloomer, we're back where we started." He could afford to smile. So could the lawyers. They could afford to bally well laugh. And all the time this poacher fellow was wondering what all the fuss was about. He never knew. He couldn't read. I could read – but I was wondering too. No, George. Appreciate the compliment – if it is a compliment – but definitely no.'

The major was very proud of his sons and took a very natural interest in their careers. Digby, the elder, became a chartered accountant. His father sniffed a little at the idea – particularly when he found that he had to read a certain amount of law for his examinations – but at any rate it was very different from being a lawyer. So, as the boy was very keen on the profession, he let him go in for it. And he did extremely well. By the time he was thirty he was making a large income. The younger son, John, became a farmer. This was entirely satisfactory. A gentleman farmer was the nearest approach to a country gentleman. And who knew but one day he might be upgraded to a country gentleman again? Meanwhile, Digby the accountant was quite useful to John the farmer, and John too made a considerable financial success of his career.

It was as a result of Digby's professional activities that Digby and John met Prunella and Jane. Digby had been called in to advise in a case in which a barrister in Prunella's chambers was concerned. He was waiting alone in the clerk's room for a conference to begin when Prunella came in. They were mutually attracted to each other and introduced themselves and, before the conference began, had made arrangements to dine together. Digby said nothing to his father. There was no point in worrying the old man. After all, there might be nothing in it – though, from the beginning, Digby had more than a faint premonition that he was going to marry this girl if she would have him.

After their acquaintanceship had lasted a few months Digby felt that John should be let into the secret. And in consequence John met Jane. Soon both brothers realised that they had started something which they intended to finish but the results of which might be disastrous for their father. They were as devoted to him as he was to them, but the idea of sacrificing their future happiness with Prunella and Jane was too high a price to pay for their devotion. The question was how to reconcile the old boy to both marriages.

It was not a simple matter at all. Their mother was entirely a yes-woman so far as the major was concerned. They knew what her reaction would be.

'But your father,' she would say. 'It would kill him.'

Well, of course, it wouldn't kill him. He was not a fat man and an apoplectic fit was out of the question. But, after his rage had subsided, it would leave him desperately unhappy. And, having nothing to do since his retirement, he would probably brood about it for the rest of his days and become an embittered old man.

The brothers' first attempt was a hopeless failure. They brought the girls to dinner at home and hoped that their natural charm and obvious intelligence might break down their father's resistance. The evening certainly began all right. Prunella and Jane looked their best, and their attractiveness was certainly not lost on the major. He insisted on handing round the drinks himself and he paid both girls pretty compliments about their dresses. Everything went splendidly until the middle of dinner. Then the major started the fateful conversation.

'And what do you do for a living, Prunella?' he asked. 'You're much too young and pretty for me to call you Miss Coombe,' he added, 'if you don't mind.'

'I should hate you to call me Miss Coombe.'

'Well, what d'you do? Or are you a lady of leisure? There are not so many of them these days. And I'm afraid even then sometimes leisure stands for something else.'

'Oh, nothing very exciting,' Prunella parried.

'Father,' interrupted Digby, 'your roses are coming on wonderfully. But what's the one with big saucer-like blooms?'

'That? Oh, we've had that for years. It's a Mermaid.'

'I love roses,' said Jane. 'Do you look after them yourself?'

'Well, I potter about a bit – but we have a man once a week. He's a nice old boy. But he knows nothing about roses. Trouble is – he seems to think he does.'

The four young people immediately began to assume an interest in roses which none of them had. They all tried to remember the name of every rose they'd ever heard of. Up and down the table they played the rose game. Fashion and Frensham, Ena Harkness and Josephine Bruce, Virgo and Message, and those attractive little things – what are they called? Suddenly there was a pause – as there must be when only one person taking part in a conversation is really interested in the subject matter. So Mrs Buttonstep stepped gallantly into the breach. That was normally her function. She seldom spoke except when everyone stopped for a moment. Then she would usually make some remark about the time of year, the vicar's last sermon, or something which she hoped would get things started again.

'You were telling us about your job, Miss Coombe,' she said, looking at Prunella.

'Prunella, please,' said Prunella. 'Yes, of course,' she added, 'but the major was telling us about his experiments with grafting. They're far more interesting. Is there a Buttonstep rose?'

'Well,' said the major, 'as a matter of fact that's in the melting pot at the moment. If you had the choice, what colours would you try to combine?'

They were all ready with suggestions and kept the conversation going for quite a time with them. Then, when it started to flag, Jane, seeing a look on Mrs Buttonstep's face which clearly showed what she would say if there were silence, turned the subject to rhododendrons. From rhododendrons they went to chrysanthemums, tried tulips, which, for some reason, the major did not care for, and – after a few unsuccessful attempts to discuss fruit and the kitchen garden – managed to find a new subject in birds. The major was not a bird-watcher, but he took sufficient interest in the subject to enable the four young people to play the bird game for quite a time. But inevitably the conversation once again flagged and once more Mrs Buttonstep referred to the fatal question.

'Yes, what do you do?' said the major. 'I shall begin to think it's something not quite nice if you keep us waiting much longer.' He had suddenly remembered that it was at least twenty minutes since he had asked the question. There was nothing for it. Prunella gulped and then tried to say in as off-hand a manner as possible: 'I'm at the Bar, as a matter of fact.'

There was a horrible silence.

'And what do *you* do?' said Mrs Buttonstep to Jane, in a genuine endeavour to improve the situation.

Jane gulped.

'As a matter of fact,' she said, 'I'm a solicitor.'

'They couldn't really help it, father,' said Digby. 'You see, their father's a judge.'

He realised instantly that it was not the right moment for this disclosure. It was like a boxer, who had landed two successful and painful body blows, delivering to his victim a swift upper-cut. As Digby's intention was to soften the blows, not to knock his father out, he regretted his haste. But it was too late for regrets. There was his father sitting at the end of the table, imagining a double wedding with the Church full of lawyers, barristers, solicitors and judges. Some people who dislike lawyers have some respect for them when they become judges. But not the major. As far as he was concerned judges were as bad as any of them. Sitting up there in their pantomime dress, mouthing unnecessarily long phrases for the sake of effect, leaning back composedly and saying 'wait a moment, please, Mr Wotherspoon,' while the witness stands in the witness box petrified, with sweat pouring down his face, just because he's said 'right' instead of 'left,' the major loathed them. He could visualise it all.

'So you meant "left" did you, Mr Wotherspoon? Then will you kindly explain to me why you said "right"? You do know the difference, I suppose, between your left hand and your right?'

'Yes, my Lord.'

'Good,' his Lordship is gracious enough to say. 'That's something.'

Sarcastic, sadistic, sententious devils, thought the major. And barristers almost as bad. At any rate they had in their favour that they were paid to be offensive, while judges were not. But the licence they were given to insult witnesses – it was intolerable.

'Come, do yourself justice, Mr Snell. You don't really mean that.'

Mr Snell did mean it. The thing had happened just as Mr Snell had said. And yet this plaguey person in a white-grey wig and black gown and preaching bands was making it appear, by his tone of voice and use of language, that no sane person could possibly have thought it happened.

'Do yourself justice, Mr Snell.' The major had actually heard the words and had never forgotten the occasion. And, if you met one of these gentry out of Court, he would calmly tell you that all he was trying to do was to elicit the truth. Elicit the truth! He was doing nothing of the kind. If he was not trying to twist it round the other way, he was at least trying to blanket it.

And solicitors. Just as bad. Not only did they feed the barristers with the ammunition with which to carry out their noisome practices in Court, but, if you consulted them alone about some perfectly ordinary subject, they would take half-an-hour to tell you that the situation was rather obscure. He remembered having once consulted the local solicitor on a question of notice. He wanted to dismiss a man. Must the week's notice expire at the end of a current week or could it expire any time?

'Now, let me see,' Mr Tweedie had said, 'let me see.'

He had paused for a few moments while he put his hands together as though he might be going to pray. Then he had announced with an air of profundity: 'It's a nice point.'

'It's not a nice point at all,' the major had said. 'It's a perfectly straightforward matter upon which I feel half-ashamed at having to consult a lawyer. But I saw your name-plate outside. Solicitor, it said, Commissioner for Oaths. I thought that meant at any rate that you knew the rudiments of law. You took examinations, didn't you?'

'A long time ago, I'm afraid,' Mr Tweedie had said. 'Longer than I like to think.'

'Then you've forgotten all your law?'

'Not all of it, I hope, but quite a lot, I'm afraid. We all do. But fortunately we know where to find it. We're not supposed to keep it all in here, you know,' he said, tapping his head. 'Some of it's over there.'

He had gone to a bookcase and taken out a book.

'Master and Servant. Notice. Ah – here we are. I think we'll have the answer to your little problem in a moment, Major Buttonstep.'

The moment had become a minute, and the minute five minutes before the major, who was patient with his family, his tradesmen, his dogs, the weather, his betting losses – indeed with everything and everyone except lawyers, had spoken.

'Well, really! How much longer?'

'It's not quite as simple as I thought,' Mr Tweedie had begun. 'You see, there's one line of authority which suggests that the position is analogous to the situation between landlord and tenant while …'

'Look here, sir,' the major had broken in, 'I have not come to you about a house or a flat or an agricultural holding. And, believe me, if that case arises, I shan't come here, or I suppose I shall be told that the case is analogous to cooks and house-parlourmaids. I haven't come here about an agricultural worker. I believe my chauffeur is stealing. I can't prove it. I don't want to be involved in lawsuits. So I want to give him notice – proper notice, legal notice, notice which won't send him running off to get legal aid and questions asked in Parliament, notice which will be effective and final and won't land me in litigation. That's all I ask, and, first of all, you tell me it's a nice point and then you talk about landlords and tenants. I wonder what would have happened to me if, when my CO had told me as adjutant to tell him how to courtmartial a man, I'd said it was a nice point or talked about analogies to this and that. He'd have had *me* courtmartialled and I should bally well have deserved it.'

'I'm very sorry, major,' Mr Tweedie had said politely, 'but it isn't always as easy as people think to state the law with certainty.'

'Well, it ought to be. But I suppose, if it were, there wouldn't be so much work for the lawyers. Well, I can't wait here all night. What's the answer?'

'Well, major, I cannot tell you definitely what the law is, though I can tell you what I think it is. I think that a week's notice at any time will do.'

'Right. Then that's what he'll get.'

'But,' Mr Tweedie had continued, 'if you want to be quite safe from the possibility of litigation, I should give him a week expiring at the end of a current week – just like in cases between landlord and tenant.'

'Confound landlords and tenants. First you say one thing and then another. But I suppose what it boils down to in the end is to give him the longer notice. All right, I'll do that. But I could have done that without coming to you.'

'I'm sorry,' said Mr Tweedie, 'but that's the safest thing to do.'

So the major had given the chauffeur a full week's notice expiring at the end of a current week. And the chauffeur had sued the major for a month's wages.

And now here were his two sons, the only successors of his line, the offspring of hundreds of gentlemen and one soldier, obviously bent on marrying into the law. And not just into the fringe of it. Right into the centre. A barrister and a solicitor – the children of a judge. Even as he sat at the dinner table, he could see his grandchildren and great-grandchildren in monstrous wigs and gowns preparing for cases, conducting cases, presiding over cases, telling decent men and women to 'do themselves justice,' impoverishing landowners with arguments which lasted weeks, months or even years, and then perhaps coming to look at his tombstone – plain, it should be – no angels or anything like that – no florid inscriptions – no 'here lies' because that was obvious and unnecessary, almost legal in its precision – just 'Claude Buttonstep late of the 1st Blankshires, son of Herbert and Henrietta Buttonstep of Buttonstep Court. Died …' Now, when would he die? His anger and distress were so great that he almost wished he could have a coronary there and then and get it over. Not out of revenge or anything like that. His love for his sons had not turned to hatred. Simply out of despair. And then he visualised his wife's grief and decided that he had better live. And then for a moment he wondered if his imagination had led him too far. Perhaps his sons had no thought of marriage. After all, you don't have to marry the girl because you bring her home to dinner with your parents. And then he looked again at the four young people. And despair regained control. The girls were so attractive. They were nice girls too. Pleasant and easy to talk to. And with good manners. Yes, marriage must be in the air. But perhaps it was not too late. If the young people's feelings had not gone too far, perhaps he could still save the day.

He said nothing till the end of dinner. Then: 'D'you mind if we reverse the procedure, my dear, and if the boys and I leave you and the girls to chat? I want to have a word with them.'

'Of course.'

He got up and Digby and John followed him to his study. As soon as they were in and he had shut the door, he said: 'Are you both serious?'

'Serious, father?'

'You know what I mean. Do you want to marry them?'

Digby looked at John. Their father saw the look, and spoke again before they could reply.

'Have you actually asked them?'

'No.'

'Thank God.'

He was silent for a moment and then he put his arms on his sons' shoulders.

'Now, you know that your mother and I only want you to be happy. But happiness does not just consist in getting married to a kind, intelligent and very attractive girl. For a few months, a few years if you like, it may seem so. But, believe me, youthful ardour cools and, although it can ripen into something far more durable, far more worthwhile than the exciting love between two young people, whether it ripens into that glorious state or not depends upon a lot of things. And tradition is one of them. Your family has hated lawyers from time immemorial. They have been bled white by them. I can even speak from experience. It cost me over fifty pounds to sack a dishonest chauffeur.'

13

'But I thought you won the case, father.'

'Of course I won the case. But it cost me over fifty pounds just the same. That's the law if you please. And the lawyers. It's not as if I acted without advice. Oh, no. In spite of my hatred of the race, I went to one before I sacked the man. I wish I hadn't. Then I could have blamed myself for what happened. But not a bit of it. "What must I do to be quite safe from litigation?" I asked the fellow. He hemmed and hawed and talked about all sorts of things I hadn't come to consult him about, landlords and tenants and Heaven knows what, but eventually I pinned him down. So he told me what I had to do to be safe – to be quite, quite safe. I did it. Cost me over fifty pounds. I might have known. It's in their blood. They can't help it, any more than a stoat can help killing a rabbit. But I don't want to have a race of bloodsuckers for my grandchildren.'

'But, father, really they're not so bad. Why don't you meet old Coombe? He's not half a bad old boy.'

'Oh, God!' said the major, 'then you really are serious. I felt it in my bones. Not half a bad old boy, did you say? Look, Digby, I'll show you something in a moment. But, before that, have you ever thought about the subject seriously? We all know the law's an ass, but we don't want it braying in our own back garden, do we? You've heard about Judge Jeffreys? You wouldn't like to have him in the family, would you? D'you think these chaps are any better?'

'Oh, come, father – they don't hang everyone.'

'No, they don't. But they'd like to. Look at the fuss they made when hanging was abolished for stealing. Have you ever read about the wailing that went on from the Bench when the Bill for abolition was introduced? Talk of prophets of doom! The judges of the time held up their hands in horror and solemnly warned Parliament that it would be impossible to tell how serious the consequences of abolition might be. Anyone who listened might have expected to have his house burgled the next day. Oh, they use more polished language today – to go with the times. But the spirit's the same. Off with his head.'

'I'm sure you wouldn't find Mr Justice Coombe like that.'

'I don't propose to find him at all, thank you,' said the major. 'My boys, do you realise what you are doing? I'm not saying a word against these two girls. They seem nice enough to me. But the law is in their blood and it's a much bigger thing than they are. D'you think these judges, who are so bloodthirsty on the Bench, are different by nature from other men? D'you think these barristers and solicitors who soak you for thousands of pounds – and then tell you how sorry they are you've lost but the judge was very difficult – d'you think they're different by nature from you and me? Of course not. It's the law itself that gets into their blood and makes them what they are. I tell you, I hate the lot. For generations our family has hated them with a bitter, permanent, implacable hatred. For God's sake don't both of you let us down.'

It was even worse than the boys had feared. They looked at each other unhappily. They had never seen their father like this before.

'You're not either of you actually engaged?'

'No, father.'

'Well, there's still hope then. Now let me show you something.'

The major took a key from his desk and opened a cupboard. It was full of dusty books and papers, some of them very old indeed.

'Look what they've done to us, these lawyers,' he said. 'We used to own three-quarters of the land round here.

15

The whole of Buttonstep village belonged to us. Now what have we got? Half an acre. And that's due to your mother. Look at these.'

The cupboard was indeed full of legal history.

'In the estate of Charles Buttonstep deceased. Bradbury v Buttonstep,' 'The Queen against Buttonstep,' 'Buttonstep v The Queen,' 'Marigold v Marigold (Buttonstep intervening),' 'Buttonstep v Buttonstep,' 'The Commissioners of Inland Revenue v Buttonstep,' 'The humble Petition of Josiah Buttonstep,' and many others.

'Look at the Courts we've been through,' said the major bitterly. 'We've done the lot. Police Court, County Court, High Court, Court of Appeal, Privy Council, House of Lords. One case alone took three years. Ever read Bleak House? That was no exaggeration. It was nothing to what our family has suffered. And now I suppose we're going to have Mr Justice Buttonstep, Lord Justice Buttonstep, My Lord Buttonstep and all the rest of it. I hope I'm dead before it happens.'

'Father, if we get married, our children might not want to be lawyers. They may hate them like you. We shan't *try* to send them into the law.'

'They won't be able to help it. The Coombe blood will be too much for them. I remember the name now. He comes from what lawyers would call a long line of distinguished judges. They were distinguished all right. One of them ruined your great-great-grandfather with a wicked judgment. Wicked, I tell you. Oh – it was upset by the House of Lords all right, and they said it was – well, they didn't call it wicked – dog don't eat dog – but they used legal language for saying that the judge was talking through his hat. Much good that was. Your great-great-grandfather was dead by then.'

16

'But, father, really! The Buttonstep blood may prove stronger than the Coombe. All our children may be like you.'

'Don't you believe it,' said the major. 'Even in the womb the lawyer will find a way. For all we know, he'll take legal proceedings in there, and the child that's born will be the result of a *nolle prosequi* or some other of their beastly Latin phrases. Why can't they talk English in an English Court? I bet half of them don't understand what they're saying. They pronounce it all wrong, anyway.'

Ten minutes later three unhappy men joined Mrs Buttonstep and the girls.

'And what sort of a man would you like to marry?' she was asking Prunella, as they came in. Prunella blushed.

'I haven't really got round to thinking about it,' she lied.

'There's plenty of time,' said the major. 'I don't believe in these boy and girl marriages. I should marry a lawyer, if I were you. That'll save a lot of trouble.'

'I think we've got enough legal blood in the family,' said Jane. 'It's time we had something different.'

'I wonder what your father would say to that,' said the major.

'Oh, he'd agree, I'm sure,' said Prunella. 'He's very broad-minded.'

'Broad-minded!' repeated the major loudly, and then remembered that he was the host.

'I mean,' said Prunella hastily, 'that he likes people for what they are, not what they do.'

Meanwhile the young men sat glumly silent. They wished they'd never brought the girls home. They should have approached it another way. What was to be done? There are still families whose members try not to hurt each other and children who, at any rate, consider their parents' wishes, even if they do not always comply with

17

them. They are possibly unfashionable, but they exist. And the Buttonsteps were such a family. Digby and John were relieved when the girls said they must go home.

They all went in the family car. After an uncomfortable silence Digby eventually said: 'I'm sorry father dislikes lawyers so much. His family's lost so much going to law.'

'I think he's sweet,' said Jane, 'and I don't blame him. We're necessary to the community – like dustmen – but I can understand people not liking us. We're terribly expensive, we sometimes take an awful time to produce very little result, and we make mistakes.'

'I wish father could have heard you say that. I'm sure he'd have been delighted.'

Just before they reached the girls' home, Digby said: 'Your father's a particularly good judge, isn't he? The papers always speak of him as if he were.'

'Well, he is as a matter of fact, at least we think so,' said Jane. 'But I shouldn't go by the papers. Any judge who's presided over a lot of famous criminal trials gets a reputation with the public. But it doesn't mean he's necessarily a good judge.'

'Could I have a word with him tonight, d'you think?' asked Digby.

'Of course. He never goes to bed till late.'

Half-an-hour later Digby was talking to Mr Justice Coombe in his study.

'I hope you'll forgive me, sir,' he said, 'if I come straight to the point.'

'It'll be a pleasant change after the day I've had in Court.'

'My father can't stand lawyers.'

'Yes?'

'Would you mind if I married Prunella, sir?'

'Would she?'

'Well, I haven't asked her yet, sir – but I hope not.'

'And you're actually asking me first? How pleasantly old-fashioned.'

'I'm afraid that wasn't the only point, sir. It's about my father. He can't bear the idea of my marrying into the law. Can you think of any way of making him change his mind? It isn't that he'd actually stop us. But he's so unhappy about it.'

'Why does he hate us all so much?'

Digby gave the judge a short account of the papers his father had shown him and what he had said about them.

'I see,' said the judge. 'You come from a very litigious family, don't you? Your father and his family may have hated the lawyers, but they've certainly been great benefactors to the profession. I should rather be inclined to think that the trouble springs from your family having lost too many cases.'

'You mean that they're really fond of litigation but that it's proved too expensive? Like a racing man gives it up because he always loses.'

'Well, you've a fair amount of evidence to support that theory.'

'And what's the cure, sir?'

'I'm afraid,' said the judge, 'that I'm not in a position to suggest a cure. With a racing man it would be different. Let him win a few bets and he'll become as keen as ever again.'

'Would you see him, sir, and have a talk with him?'

'Certainly, if he'd see me.'

'Yes, that's the trouble,' said Digby. 'I don't think he would. But, leaving him out of it for a moment, sir, if Prunella would marry me would it be all right with you?'

'I expect so,' said the judge, 'but I haven't known you very long, have I? I'm usually ready to back my girls' judgment – perhaps Jane's rather more than Prunella's –

though I don't think either of them would make a really bad mistake.'

'Thank you, sir,' said Digby. 'I am grateful to you for being so nice about it.'

CHAPTER TWO

The Buttonstep Arms

On the way home Digby and John discussed ways and means of trying to reconcile their father to a double wedding. Meanwhile he was unburdening himself to his wife. She was a great comfort to him, always sympathetic, always agreeing – with never, apparently, a thought of her own. Some men would have found her insipid but she was just right for the major. When he was worried she treated him as if he were a child that had fallen down, and usually it soothed him wonderfully.

'I don't think I could bear it,' he said to her. 'Will you speak to them? I mean I'm not a particularly narrow minded man. If they'd been a bookmaker's or a fishmonger's daughters I shouldn't have minded, provided they were respectable. But inbred lawyers! I ask you. I expect their mother was in the game too. I ought to have asked.'

'I think they said she'd been a journalist or something. I'm not sure.'

'A law reporter, you can bet,' said the major.

'They aren't actually married yet, dear. Suppose we have those two nice girls we met last summer to dinner as a distraction?'

'Too obvious, I'm afraid, but it's nice of you to suggest it. No – somehow or other we've got to bring home to the boys that lawyers are just outside the pale, that you soil your hands if you shake theirs and your lips if you talk to them.'

'They seemed very clean girls, dear.'

'Yes, yes, of course. Not literally. As you say, they *were* clean girls – attractive too.'

'If only they'd been fishmongers.'

'Exactly. I've no objection to the girls themselves. On the contrary. But it's the idea of getting law into the Buttonstep blood that horrifies me. I imagine that a Hindu asked to eat beef would feel much the same.'

'We must see what we can do,' said his wife encouragingly.

'But what? I'd hate to make either of the boys unhappy, and I'm sure they feel the same about us. But the thought is too terrible. The next thing we'll find is Buttonstep & Buttonstep Solicitors, Thomas Buttonstep, QC, Mr Justice Buttonstep. Just think what my grandfather would have said. A lawyer in the family. We've had some queer fish from time to time, mark you, and I'm not saying we're any better than other families. There was old Archie Buttonstep, who did three years for something or other, and the Marigold Divorce case. Mary Buttonstep got away with it, but I'm not at all sure that she ought to have. Those letters were pretty damning. Which reminds me – I've promised to do a new edition of the case. Oh, well, it can wait. I can't do anything till this crisis is over. I think I'll go and have a chat with Archie Randall in the morning. He's a sensible fellow. Might think of something.'

'Yes, you do that, dear.'

Archibald Randall was the licensee of the Buttonstep Arms. It was an attractive old inn which he had enlarged and modernised, but he still maintained the original sign outside. It was very weatherworn and efforts at restoration made some fifty years previously had not been satisfactory. He had to replace the name altogether but the rest of it was at least two hundred years old. From the road you could see practically nothing except the name. But if you took a pair of steps and climbed up you could just see the outline of the single step and the button resting upon it. It was a large button, almost the size of a small plate; indeed, but for the name, most people would have thought it was a plate. The sign was not taken from the coat of arms of the Buttonsteps, which was entirely different and had no relation either to steps or buttons. Their motto was *In Veritate Salus*, which the major would quite unfairly use as being one of the reasons for his family disliking lawyers. He supported to the full the common but erroneous idea that lawyers have no regard for the truth whatsoever.

Archie was a well-educated man who had taken to hotel-keeping late in life. He had a flair for it, one of his assets being a prodigious memory. This, though useful in any job, is not more necessary for a hotel-keeper than for anyone else. But in Archie's case it enabled him to run a bookmaker's business at the same time. It was entirely illegal but added to his profits and, being illegal, was not subject to tax. The reason why he was never prosecuted was simple. There were no betting slips. Every bet was retained in Archie's mind. If the local policeman had seen betting slips being handed over he would have been bound to report the matter, the place would have been raided, betting slips and other written evidence of a betting business would have been. found and Archie would have been prosecuted, convicted, and would have lost his licence. But, as everything was done entirely by word of mouth, there was no evidence of any kind, except of a whispered conversation. Now, of course, it would have been possible to set a trap for Archie and for two strangers to enter into the village life and eventually give the necessary evidence to obtain a conviction. But that is not the way the law is enforced in the ordinary English village. If the local policeman sees the law is being broken in one of the normal ways, or if he has reason to suspect that there is the normal evidence of a crime available, he either makes a charge himself or reports the matter to his superior officer. But, although the Buttonstep constable knew perfectly well what Archie was doing, the decencies were observed when he entered the inn and either the conversation was switched to something else or the voices dropped to a whisper, and the constable, having the right instincts, never dreamed of trying to listen in.

Of course, at first people were a little shy of doing betting business without any records being made. But, when they found that Archie never made a mistake, they soon completely trusted him. At the beginning one or two of the less scrupulous customers tried to bluff Archie. But quite unavailingly. He never refused to pay on a winner but he never paid on a loser. As gambling losses are irrecoverable, the industry depends to a large extent on trust and, in consequence, it is not so surprising to find that people whose faces and manner would not normally lead you to trust them with sixpence can be completely relied upon to pay their losses to the full. It is not that they are people of such nice consciences but simply that they could not exist in the trade unless they were completely trusted. And the only way to be completely trusted is to be completely trustworthy. Racing men rightly say that, whereas in ordinary business everything is normally written down and often long and (to the layman)

24

unintelligible contracts are signed in transactions involving only quite small amounts, in the racing world many thousands of pounds are staked by word of mouth only and the parties are entirely dependent upon one or another's honesty. This is true enough but the reason for it is simply that betting could not otherwise exist in this country. There are, of course, some defaulters and fraud is sometimes practised. But the average bookmaker and punter, though not in the rest of their lives necessarily conspicuous for their reliability, are completely honest in their betting transactions.

Archie made full use of this phenomenon and, as soon as it was realised that in the space of five minutes he could take a dozen sometimes quite complicated bets from different people without getting any of them mixed up, they used him like a betting shop. Indeed, if one of them did not make a private note of his wager in his diary and himself made a mistake, he would accept Archie's word without question. The brain is a remarkable machine and it would have been most interesting had it been possible to see how Archie stored the information as certainly as though each bet had been duly written down and recorded in duplicate.

When the major went in for a drink the following evening, Archie was taking a few bets for the next day. He looked up for a moment to see who had come in and, after a cordial 'good evening' to the major, continued with his illegal transactions. As soon as they were over he turned his attention to the major.

'I sometimes wonder why the bookmakers in Copplestone don't try to close you down,' said the major. Copplestone was the nearest town to the village of Buttonstep.

'Close me down!' said Archie. 'Not on your life. There are only two of them, and they get quite a bit of business, as I lay it off with them. If I didn't take these bets no one would. Think of all that money lying idle. Horrible. Or they might use it for football pools. Close me down indeed! They'd offer to share the costs of my defence if anyone else tried to.'

'I see,' said the major. 'Well, get me a pound on Simply Splendid, will you?'

'I will if you like,' said Archie, 'but you might as well tear the money up. It hasn't a hope against Barrister-at-Law.'

The major took a pound note out of his wallet and tore it into halves and then quarters.

'That's how I feel about Barrister-at-Law,' he said. 'I wouldn't back it if I had second sight and *knew* it was going to win. Let's have a bit of Sellotape, Archie, to stick this thing together again.'

Archie fetched the tape from an adjoining room and the major stuck the note together again.

'I think you go too far, major,' said Archie. 'I don't much care for lawyers myself, but if one of them could do me a bit of good, I shouldn't say no.'

For answer the major tore the note in half again.

'Steady, major,' said Archie. 'I'll run out of Sellotape if you go on at this rate.'

'My boy Digby wants to marry a lawyer, and as if that weren't enough so does John.'

'Well, they can't both marry her. That's something.'

'There are two of them.'

'Oh, that's hard. On the other hand, it'll be quite useful to have a couple in the family. I dare say they'd advise you for nothing.'

'I don't want any advice, thank you – not from lawyers anyway. But it's not true that I don't want advice – how can I stop it?'

'Well, they're over twenty-one – so you can't get them made wards of court.'

'Oh – I don't mean that way. Shouldn't dream of trying it. What, fight my own sons in the Law Courts! Not likely. They're good boys, Digby and John. Why do they have to go and fall for a couple of lawyers? No, I want to find some way of persuading them – some way of showing them that Buttonsteps just can't marry into the legal profession. Now you had a bit of trouble with Alice over that architect fellow, and it came out all right in the end. Can you give me any suggestions?'

'But it wasn't his job in that case, major. It was the fellow himself. We managed to get Alice to see that he wasn't the right type for her.'

'Lawyers aren't the right type for anyone.'

'I know what you feel, major, but I must say that, if the girls were all right, I shouldn't worry what their job is. After all, they'll give it up probably when they marry.'

'I thought you'd understand better, Archie. If you wanted a Derby winner there are some sires and some dams which you wouldn't breed from at any price, aren't there?'

'That's true.'

'Well, just as horses may bring sprinting or staying power into the blood, so do human beings bring special characteristics. These two girls come from a long line of the legal fraternity. Aren't the children going to want to be lawyers? There's a good chance of it anyway, isn't there? Look at lawyers' names. The same ones are always cropping up. It isn't nepotism, it's because they've got it in their blood. Just imagine a Buttonstep a lawyer. He'd have to change the family motto. Safety in truth! With a lawyer! I thought you'd be more sympathetic.'

'Well, I'm terribly sorry, major, but I must say I think there are far worse people than lawyers.'

'Who?'

Archie didn't answer at once.

'There's no profession which takes so much from you and gives you so little in return,' said the major. 'Dammit, there are bad chaps in every job. I'm not saying that there aren't decent people among the lawyers. Of course there are. They're decent as people, but they can't be as lawyers. Everyone else does something for you – the architect, the surveyor, the accountant, the doctor – everyone gives real value for what you pay him – all except the lawyer. Sometimes they don't completely ruin you – as they have our family – but they charge the earth and do nothing constructive whatever. The architect leaves you with a house, the accountant with a balance sheet, the doctor with a new tummy: all the lawyer leaves you with is a bill of costs. They're parasites.'

'Oh – come, major!'

'Well, what worse profession is there? Criminals, I suppose you'll say. Well, I'll grant you that. But crime isn't yet recognised as a profession. If there were degrees in larceny and housebreaking I'd allow that lawyers – some of them, anyway, were better. It just shows how far you have to stoop to find anyone to compare lawyers with.'

'I really didn't know you felt so strongly on the subject.'

'Well, I haven't had to say as much up till now, but this business has brought it to a head. Who was it said: "Let's kill all the lawyers"? Pity he didn't.'

'Well, if you tell the boys how strongly you feel on the subject, they may give up the idea for your sake.'

'But I don't want that, Archie. They'd resent it in the end. We're good friends in our family and I don't want sacrifices made for me. I want to find some way which will make them change their minds of their own accord. I want some person or thing suddenly to show them the light – to show them that they just can't go on with it. Surely you can think of something?'

'If you can't, it's not likely that I can. I suppose you could collect a list of some of the lawyers in the last fifty years who've gone to the bad.'

'You could do that with any profession, Archie. There are no more criminals among the lawyers than among accountants and doctors. I want them to feel that it's like a devout Roman Catholic marrying a heathen. He just can't do it.'

'Haven't you said that to them?'

'Well, I suppose I have really, in a way. But it didn't seem to make any difference.'

'Well, I'll think it over, major, and, if I have any bright ideas, I'll let you know next time you come in. Now what about that bet? Which is it to be? Barrister-at-Law is a certainty. I'm laying off every penny that comes in.'

'Barrister-at-Law!' said the major, and once again tore the note into half. 'And that goes for Mr Justice Coombe, too,' he said. 'Pass me the Sellotape, old boy.'

CHAPTER THREE

Wig and Pen

Mr Justice Coombe was one of the most able judges ever to sit in the Queen's Bench Division. He had been educated at a public school and Cambridge. At Cambridge he spent one year on getting a first in the Classical tripos. He then turned to Science, a subject in which he had only been slightly grounded at school. In two years he got a first in part one of the Mechanical Sciences tripos. He stayed on another year and read law. He took a first in part one of the Law tripos. During those four years he had been taking a full part in University life, getting two blues and writing part of the Footlights May Week Show. He also played the violin in his College orchestra. But he still had time to kiss two girls from Newnham and one from Girton.

During one vacation he had been introduced to a High Court judge, Mr Justice Remnant, who had invited him to sit with him on the Bench when he went on Circuit. Mr Justice Remnant was not a particularly good judge and had the bad judicial habit of trying to fit the facts of every case to such law as he knew, rather than to find out what the facts were and then to learn the law on the subject if he did not already know it. Usually he did this quite unconsciously, but Edward Coombe soon noticed the tendency. A question might arise as to whether a notice had been given on a particular day. If it had been, then one side was clearly entitled to succeed. If it had not, a difficult point of law emerged, and the judge would have had to deal with this before he could decide in favour of either party. No such point of law ever arose while Edward Coombe sat with the judge. On one occasion the judge even commented on it: 'Bit of luck, my boy,' he said, 'I decided the facts as I did. Otherwise it'd have thrown the whole Assize out. I should never have got to Chester by Monday, or I'd have had to leave this case unfinished – a thing I hate doing. You remember that, my boy, when you're a judge. Take care of the facts and the law will take care of itself.'

'Thank you,' said Edward Coombe, 'I'll certainly remember it.'

And he did, deciding that a bad example was almost as useful a guide as a good one, provided you knew which was bad and which was good.

He was interested to find that even he, a young man with no professional experience of the law and little theoretical knowledge, could sometimes spot obvious errors in the tactics or advocacy on the part of counsel.

After he had been called to the Bar he was introduced into the chambers of a successful junior. There he read for a year as a pupil and at the end of it was asked to stay on as a member of chambers. After ten years he took silk, and as a QC he swept everything before him.

His capacity for spotting mistakes developed rapidly as his practice increased, and one of his great assets at the Bar was the way in which he could tell that something was missing from a case. It might be that it was his own client who was concealing something from him, it might be that it was the litigant on the other side or a third party who did not want the full truth to be known. But, when Edward Coombe said: 'There's something behind all this which no one wants to tell us,' he was seldom, if ever, wrong. He retained this quality when he became a judge and sometimes surprised both sides by showing them that neither of them was telling the true story.

Mr Justice Coombe married comparatively late in life – not one of the three girls he kissed at Cambridge, but a woman novelist who wrote excellent crime stories which were almost entirely inaccurate in technical legal details. The judge had read all of them before he met her but it was only after they were married that, in the course of casual conversation, she learned that every book she had written was full of legal errors.

'Why d'*you* mind?' he asked. '*I* didn't mind in the least. They were rattling good stories and the fact that both counsel in your last book would probably have been disbarred for unprofessional behaviour and the solicitors struck off the Rolls didn't spoil it for me in the least. I was interested in the plot and the professional details could go hang as far as I was concerned. Why shouldn't you call it a witness *stand* if you want to? After all, the witness stands there, and it isn't a box as it has no lid. Though on the whole it wouldn't be a bad idea to have a lid for some witnesses.'

'But I made counsel walk up to the witness and shake his fist in her face.'

'A jolly good thing too. She was lying like a trooper.'

'And the judge asked the prisoner if he'd ever tried to murder anyone else in that way before.'

'If he hadn't, the chap might have been acquitted and I couldn't have borne that.'

'But you will help me get things right in the future?'

'If you wish, my dear, of course. But I much prefer them as they are. Why try to write the things that really happen? There are enough of those in the world in all conscience. Write about the things that don't happen. They're much more exciting and amusing.'

Hester Coombe had fallen in love three times in her life. The first time it was a riding master, the second, a driving instructor and the third time it was Edward Coombe. The riding master was purely animal. The driving instructor was rather different. In the intervals between explaining the use of gears and clutch and so forth he recited poetry to her. He was very good-looking, with fair hair, and he was a born teacher. He taught first steps in driving and first steps in love with equal facility.

'How am I doing?' she asked him once.

'I'm glad to say pretty badly,' he replied. 'You'll need a lot more lessons. Take the next on the right. It's a cul-de-sac.'

In the cul-de-sac he asked her to marry him but somehow or other she managed to say 'no,' in spite of herself. She was in love all right, but she knew that there were other essential ingredients for a happy marriage besides smooth gear-changing, and she doubted if they existed in this case. The driving instructor took his defeat very well. After all, quite a number of his pupils failed.

It was not for a long time after that episode that Hester found her husband. And in the meantime she contented herself with enjoying life unmarried. She felt sure she would marry one day and she was prepared to wait much longer. Soon she started to write and gradually the tone of the letters of rejection began to sound more encouraging. Of course, if the letter came from someone to whom she had been introduced, she discounted such sentences as: 'I have read your ms with much pleasure and very much hope that you may find a publisher for it. Unfortunately we have such a tight schedule here that I do not see how we could consider it for publication within a reasonable time and it would not be fair to keep the ms so long.'

She felt sure that every publisher, however tight his schedule, would gladly loosen it a bit if anything really worthwhile came along from a new author.

But eventually she had a letter which simply said:

Dear Madam,
I should like to see you about your ms.
Yours faithfully,
Arnold Bulmer.

The fact that no time or date was suggested in no way lessened the thrill which she had on reading the letter. There were only nine effective words in it but she read them at least half-a-dozen times and kept on saying to herself: 'It can't be because he wants to hand it back to me. I sent a stamped addressed envelope. Perhaps he wants me to re-write it. Perhaps he wants to discuss terms. Or is he just a kind man who wants to encourage me?'

She telephoned Mr Bulmer's secretary to make an appointment. It was a great moment when she dialled the number of Lanson and Bollinger. She was actually telephoning a firm of publishers! They might be *her* publishers.

'This is Miss Fountain speaking,' she said. 'Might I speak to Mr Bulmer's secretary?'

'Miss who did you say?'

'Miss Fountain.'

'Is it about the job?'

'Job? Oh – no – I sent in a manuscript to Mr Bulmer and he said he would like to see me.'

'Oh,' the voice sounded less interested, 'Mr Bulmer's secretary isn't available, I'm afraid. I'll put you through to Miss Fish. Hold on, please.'

Hester waited a short time, then there was a click and a female voice said: 'Fish speaking. Who is it?'

'I don't suppose you know my name, but ...'

'That's why I asked who you were,' put in Miss Fish.

'I'm sorry. I'm Hester Fountain.'

'I'm afraid I'm none the wiser.'

'I had a letter from Mr Bulmer.'

'Is it about the job?'

'No, about a manuscript.'

'Can you do typing and shorthand?'

'Well, yes, but – '

'Mr Bulmer will see you at once. Come to the third floor and ask for me. Fish is the name. Goodbye.'

Puzzled, but glad that she was at any rate to have her interview, Hester took a taxi to Lanson and Bollinger, went up to the third floor and asked for Miss Fish.

'That's me,' said a short attractive woman, whose mind was as neat as her appearance.

'If you come here, I'm known as Fish – not Miss Fish – just plain Fish, d'you understand? And no "c" in it if you write to me. Fish – the stuff you eat – with or without chips. I'm not being funny. I like to get things straight before we start.'

'But I've come about a book.'

'Everyone comes here about books. We're publishers. This way, please.'

She was led along a corridor and then Miss Fish opened a door and showed her into Mr Bulmer's room. He was sitting at his desk writing a letter. Without looking up he said: 'Sit down, please. Thank you, Fish.'

Miss Fish went, and Hester sat down.

After about a minute, Mr Bulmer, still without looking up, said: 'I see you can spell. Or did someone correct it for you?'

'No. I can spell.'

'Married?'

'No.'

'Engaged?'

'No.'

Mr Bulmer looked up for a moment at Hester, and then went on with his letter. After another moment or so he spoke again: 'Your book's about a shorthand typist who's chased around the office by her boss.'

'That does come into it,' said Hester, who fortunately remembered that two minor characters did play a scene of that kind. She had indeed hesitated whether to cut out the scene altogether but, having been told by a friend that a little sex always improved a book, she left it in with some hesitation – as it was completely irrelevant to the plot.

'I take it you know all about being a secretary?'

'I have been one – but what I wrote is not based on experience.'

'You haven't been chased, you mean?'

'Well – not chased.'

'Is being chased what you consider one of the perquisites of a secretary?'

'I've never thought about it.'

'There's no chasing in this office, I'm afraid, except by Fish. She does any chasing there is to be done.'

'But I came about my book.'

'That's what I'm talking about, isn't it? A book about a secretary, which means you can do shorthand and typing, and you can spell. Would you like the job? No Saturdays, ten guineas, three weeks' holiday but, as I said, no chasing.'

'But my book – isn't it any good?'

'Your book's fine. It's brought the two of us together. When would you like to start?'

'But are you going to publish it?'

Mr Bulmer looked up.

'Oh, be reasonable, my dear young lady. We couldn't possibly publish it. It's not that type of book. I've a report on it here. Want to see it? You won't like it.'

He handed Hester a flimsy sheet of paper on which was typed:

Man Alive
by
Hester Fountain

Shorthand typist finds dead body. For no obvious reason does not go to police and becomes suspected. In Chapter 17 she is chased round the room by her boss. The rest of the book is fit for children but it is not a children's book.

'I see,' said Hester. 'Have you read it, by any chance?'

'Good gracious no,' said Mr Bulmer. 'On that report! What d'you take me for?'

'I take you,' said Hester, 'for a man who badly needs a secretary. If you'll read my book – properly, I mean, and give me your genuine opinion about it, I'll take the job. Otherwise, good afternoon.'

'You've got references, I suppose? I mean you haven't been to gaol or anything?'

'No. I'm quite respectable.'

'Good. Then you can start straight away? Perhaps you can do this confounded letter. I've written three pages already and the girl downstairs won't be able to read a word of it. Ready? Oh, you haven't a notebook.'

He rang a bell.

'Are you going to read my book?' asked Hester.

'I've an awful lot to read,' said Mr Bulmer. 'Stuff we're going to publish, I mean. I'll have to read it if you insist, because I really can't get a secretary who can spell. I have to work for my living. I've a wife and three children to support – oh, all right, I'll read it.'

And two months later Hester had the great pleasure of typing out her own contract for its publication. After that she stayed on as Mr Bulmer's secretary, but writing books in her spare time. They were quite successful, and it was in consequence of her winning a prize for the best crime story of the year that she met her future husband. It was at the annual dinner of a society formed by writers of criminal fiction. Edward Coombe, who had recently taken silk, had been invited to propose the health of the society, and Hester had also been invited in view of her successful story. They sat next to each other and were soon talking so much to each other that they both began to have consciences about the other people next to them.

He started the conversation in a conventional pleasing way.

'I'm so glad to have the chance of meeting someone who has given me so much pleasure. Thank you very much. I've read them all.'

'Oh, how nice of you – but you can't have. There are eight, you know.'

'I can tell you their titles if you don't believe me.'

'How wonderful.'

'Oddly enough, I started with your third or fourth and I've only just read your first – *Man Alive*, wasn't it? Did you have any difficulty in getting it published?'

'Indeed I did. I had to blackmail a publisher into taking it.'

'Excuse me, Mr Coombe,' said Edward's neighbour on the other side, 'might I ask you a legal question?'

'Of course. I can't promise an accurate answer.'

'Oh, I'm sure you can. It's quite simple. Can you be convicted of murder if the body can't be found?'

'Oh, certainly. Proof may be difficult, but there's no law that a body has to be produced.'

'But I thought they always produced a little bit anyway.'

'They do if they can. But, if someone pushed a man overboard and the body wasn't found, it wouldn't be very satisfactory if the murderer couldn't be charged.'

'But he mightn't be a murderer. The person might turn up years later.'

'That's theoretically possible, I suppose. But you can't have absolute certainty in criminal matters. If there were a reasonable chance that a person was still alive probably a man might be acquitted. But, before he was charged, every effort would be made to see if the person could have been saved.'

'Mr Coombe,' said Hester, 'I overheard what you said. I'm so grateful to you. In my next book the judge was going to throw a case out because the body couldn't be found. You see – they found a body and everyone thinks it's the man who's supposed to have been murdered. And then, at the last moment, it's proved that it's someone quite different. But the other man *was* murdered, if you see what I mean, but they can't find the body. What d'you think I ought to do?'

'You write it just as it is, Miss Fountain. I'd only spoil it for you.'

Six months later Hester celebrated the publication of *Wrong Body* by becoming engaged to Edward, and they were married shortly afterwards. He was then forty-two, and Hester thirty-five. Prunella and Jane were born three years later.

CHAPTER FOUR

Daughters of a Judge

They were identical twins but there was some difference between them intellectually. Jane had something of her father's brain, while Prunella inherited her mother's. As they grew up the question of careers arose. Jane said she wanted to be a solicitor. This was mainly due to the fact that a neighbour of theirs called Maggs was a solicitor, and a great friend of the twins. The stories he told them about a country solicitor's life were not particularly exciting, but Jane found them enthralling. He never had any murder cases, or anything of that sort: the only crimes he told them about were cases of no rear lamps on bicycles or occasionally chicken stealing. Alternatively he told them about wills and leases, and matters of that kind.

'Why d'you have to have a lawyer for all these things?' Jane asked him once. 'If I made a will, I'd just say "Everything to Pru." Wouldn't that be all right?'

'Well, if it were properly witnessed, yes,' said Mr Maggs, 'but some wills are more complicated and then it's easy to make a mistake. Sometimes, though, it's we who make the mistake. A clerk of mine once left out two lines from a will. That lost someone £3,000.'

'Did you have to pay it?'

'Oh dear no,' said Mr Maggs. 'The person who ought to have paid it was the person who had the money instead. But he hung on to it.'

'Did he take your clerk out to dinner?' asked Jane.

'He didn't even do that.'

'How mean,' said Jane.

'Of course the clerk didn't do it on purpose,' said Mr Maggs.

'But why didn't you have to pay?' asked Jane. 'It seems very unfair of the law if you didn't.'

'I didn't have to pay because there was no one who could make me,' said Mr Maggs. 'You see, I had no duty to the man who should have had the £3,000. He wasn't my client. If I gave you a diamond necklace to give to someone, and you lost it by carelessness, the person who was going to get it couldn't sue you.'

'But you could.'

'Oh, yes, I could.'

'Then what about the will? Why couldn't the person who'd made the will sue you?'

'Because he wasn't here. He was dead. If he had been alive and discovered the mistake he could have altered it and so it wouldn't have mattered.'

'It seems very strange,' said Jane.

'I know,' said Mr Maggs. 'But, you see, the dead man couldn't sue me and, although his executors could have done so, they hadn't lost anything as a result of the mistake. The estate wasn't any the worse off. The £3,000 was to have gone to Jones. Instead it went to Brown. The estate wouldn't have had it anyway. The only possible loss was a sentimental one. If, for example, the executors had been great friends of Jones and didn't like Brown – they'd have wanted the money to go to Jones and have been sorry that it didn't. But you can't get damages just for being sorry. If you could, the courts would have nothing else to do. We're all sorry sometimes.'

'Didn't you feel you ought to pay Mr Jones?'

'Well, in a way I did,' said Mr Maggs, 'but not strongly enough. I did what I could to get Brown to pay. I showed him conclusively that it was a mistake and that the man who made the will wanted Jones to have it. All he said was: "What's the law?" "Well, strictly by law you get it." "OK," he said. "Then I have it. Hand it over." '

'What a horrid person,' said Prunella.

'Have you made any other mistakes?' asked Jane.

'Well, that wasn't my personal mistake. But good gracious me, yes. Everyone makes mistakes. But carelessness is another matter.'

'I think,' said Jane, 'if I were a solicitor I should always read the will to the man who was making it before he signed it.'

'But there are pages of it sometimes. He might die first. At any rate, he often wouldn't listen, and it would tire out some old people. What we do is to give them a draft for them to read at leisure and approve or alter. Then we make a fair copy or, as we call it, make an engrossment of the approved draft.'

'Then surely you ought to read it yourself?' Jane said.

'As a matter of fact, young lady,' said Mr Maggs, 'since the unfortunate case of Mr Jones I always do. But I'm sure if you came into partnership with me I could safely leave matters like that to you.'

'We will consider your offer, Mr Maggs,' said Jane.

'I hope the decision will be favourable,' said Mr Maggs.

As Jane was then only fourteen Mr Maggs had the chances of retiring and dying before she became qualified, and he took both. But Jane had made up her mind that that was the profession for her. The question then arose as to whether Prunella should join her in partnership and for a time that was looked upon as the obvious course, for nothing would have induced the twins to be completely separated by their jobs. They realised that marriage would have that result and accepted that possibility philosophically, but a job was quite different. There was no reason why they should not work together as they had all their lives.

When they were just sixteen their father took them to the Law Courts and it was there that the idea of Prunella becoming a barrister first emerged.

'You'd look charming in one of those, Pru,' whispered Jane as they saw a tall, lean girl addressing their father.

'So would you, Jane,' said Prunella.

'Solicitors don't wear them. Look.'

She pointed to the man crouched behind Miss Edge, the tall lean barrister, and breathing hard down the back of her neck.

'Father says he's the solicitor or the solicitor's clerk.'

'He doesn't seem to think much of Miss Edge.'

Prunella was quite right. Miss Edge was the niece of the plaintiff and he had asked his solicitors to brief her. Before the case the plaintiff thought that barristers were much the same as taxis, that it didn't make much difference which you had and that he might as well give his niece a helping hand. After the case he knew better.

'But, Miss Edge,' said Mr Justice Coombe, as gently as he could, 'you haven't pleaded negligence.'

'Oh, my Lord,' said Miss Edge, but could not think how to continue.

'Oh, my God!' said Miss Edge's solicitor.

After an uncomfortable pause, he muttered at Miss Edge: 'Ask for leave to amend.'

'Would your Lordship grant leave to amend?' Before the judge could reply, a fierce little man on the other side jumped up and said: 'I shall object most strongly,' and sat down again, with a bump, as though to emphasise the strength of his objection.

'It is rather late in the day Miss Edge,' said the judge. 'After all, the plaintiff and the defendant have both given their evidence and now you're seeking to change the whole basis of the plaintiff's case. Would that be fair at this stage?'

If Miss Edge could have shrivelled into nothing she would have been happy to do so. But, as it was, all she could do was to remain standing, still tall and lean and feeling leaner and taller. The poor girl felt that everyone was looking at her, as indeed they were, and she hadn't the faintest idea what to do or say. Her solicitor was getting redder and redder in the face and saying unmentionable things to himself. It was only for about ten seconds that Miss Edge stood Cortez-like (except that she was lean) but it seemed to her at least a minute and she knew that a minute was a very long time.

'You could do better than that, Pru,' said Jane, and from that moment they discussed the possibility of Jane becoming a solicitor and feeding Prunella with briefs. The more they talked about it the more they liked the idea. Their father realised that it would be better for Jane to become the barrister and Prunella the solicitor, and said so as diplomatically as possible. But Jane was determined to become a solicitor and, that being the case, the only question was whether Prunella should join her in that profession or go to the Bar. Eventually the twins decided on the Bar. So Prunella was called to the Bar at about the same time as Jane was admitted as a solicitor.

CHAPTER FIVE

Growing Pains

The public which goes to law is remarkably long-suffering. Presumably it is much the same as the patient under an anaesthetic. He does not know what is happening round him. But, even when he does, he hardly seems resentful. It is a fact that on one occasion a young barrister of twenty-one travelled together with his solicitor and his lay client to conduct a case in what was then called a Police Court. It was a matrimonial dispute and the young barrister had read in a blue book called *Stone's Justices' Manual* words which encouraged him enormously. Indeed, the statement of the law in that authoritative work made it plain to the young man that his client was bound to succeed. He was unwise enough to confide this to his companions. They were naturally delighted and arrived at the Court in a state of happy expectation. Indeed, had there been a refreshment car on the train, it is possible that they might have celebrated the victory in advance. But the absence of this amenity did not prevent them from having uproarious jokes at their opponent's expense.

'Just imagine,' said the young man, 'there they are on the way to the Court just as we are, hoping they're going to win, and they don't know that it's legally impossible for them to do so. Ha, ha, ha.'

'Ha, ha, ha,' said the solicitor.

'Ha, ha, ha,' replied the lay client. 'Lucky we've got you on our side.'

'Oh, it's nothing,' said the young man modestly. Now, the edition of *Stone's Justices' Manual* which the young man took to Court was not actually the latest. But very nearly. It was the last but one. The young man had just wondered whether conceivably the law had been changed in that year, but the temptation to encourage his clients made him dismiss that thought from his mind at an early stage. However, when he arrived at the Court he thought he would just make certain. To his horror he found that the law had indeed been changed, but he had no time to tell his clients the bad news before the case came on. He duly lost it. Outside the Court he explained the reason to his clients. The lay client took it very well on the whole. All he said, as he said goodbye to the young man, was: 'Next time, son, get the latest edition.'

Prunella had not had the same unfortunate experience for her first brief. Jane had delivered it to her chambers personally.

'You ought to have gone to the Bar really, Jane,' said Prunella. 'You've got the confidence. I shall just get up and cry.'

'Well, we can't change now, Pru. Much too expensive. But you're quite right, really. You'd do very well as a solicitor, and I shouldn't be as frightened as you. Still, you stood up to father over the Bradbury boy.'

'That wasn't in Court. I'd really be petrified to appear in front of him. D'you think I'll have to?'

'I hope so. One day. But we shan't send you to the High Court just yet – not to the Queen's Bench Division anyway. We might try an undefended divorce before one of the milder commissioners.'

'How can you be sure it will be one of the milder ones? Supposing it were Postlethwaite?'

Jane looked serious for a moment.

'Yes, that would be grim,' she said.

Mr Commissioner Postlethwaite tried undefended divorce cases as though they were defended. It had been said of him that his view was that, if both parties to a marriage wanted it to end, he was there to see that it did not. This was not strictly true, but it is not surprising that anxious husbands and wives, for whom a decree nisi of divorce meant so much, felt that that was what the commissioner was doing. It was difficult for them to appreciate that all he was doing was to discharge to the best of his ability the duties which Parliament had imposed on him. But, with tens of thousands of divorces being granted every year, it is hard for George – who wants to marry Mary – to understand why the commissioner should appear to want to create difficulties. George's wife Hilda wants a divorce too, and wants to marry Henry. Both ladies are about to have babies, and the only obstacle to happiness all round is Mr Commissioner Postlethwaite and his interminable questions, such as: 'Is there any bargain between you about costs?'

Perhaps, when the babies grow up, they will persuade Parliament to allow divorce by consent, at any rate for marriages which have been made in a registry office. Meantime, Mr Commissioner Postlethwaite will continue to cause alarm and despondency among those who want divorces and the young counsel who appear in front of him.

When Prunella did eventually have a case in front of him, she came off pretty badly. It was a simple enough case but, though she had practised with Jane at home how not to ask leading questions, the tradition of the Divorce

Bar was too much for her and, in spite of the commissioner's increasing protests, she found it impossible not to put words into the witness' mouth the whole time, such as: 'Did he then leave you?' instead of 'Which of you left the other?' At the end of the case the erupting commissioner was still smouldering, and when Prunella said: 'Upon that evidence, my Lord, I ask for a decree nisi,' the commissioner replied: 'As you, rather than your client, have given all the evidence, perhaps you'd like me to grant the decree nisi to you as well.'

Her very first brief had been in the County Court before a registrar. He tries small cases just like a judge: well something like a judge anyway.

'Are there any snags, Jane?' asked Prunella.

'I can't think of any. All you have to do is go and ask for judgment with costs.'

'Suppose he won't give it to me?'

'He will have to.'

'Well, I know and you know – but suppose he doesn't?'

'He can't help himself. It's laid down.'

'Oh, well, I suppose you know.'

So Prunella went down to her first County Court and she created quite a stir in the robing-room. She was quite the prettiest girl that had been to Ladbroke County Court, and there were two of her, for, before she robed, no one not intimately acquainted with them could have told the difference between the two sisters.

'What's this registrar like?' she asked a young man.

'I don't know him myself, as a matter of fact, but I'm told he's all right. A bit deaf, I believe.'

'I know him quite well,' said another. 'Very decent chap, but a stickler for the rules. He doesn't know them, but he'd like to.'

'Are there any rules in my case, Jane?' asked Prunella anxiously.

'I don't think so,' said Jane, without quite the same certainty she had shown when she delivered the brief. 'You just want judgment.'

'Is yours a disposal, may I ask?' asked a solicitor.

'I beg your pardon?' said Prunella.

'A disposal … oh, excuse me …' a face had appeared at the door, and the solicitor hurried out as Prunella said: 'What's that?' She turned quickly to the barrister who had said he knew the registrar well.

'What's a disposal?' she asked.

'Haven't the faintest idea,' was the reply. 'D'you know what a disposal is?' he asked his neighbour.

'A disposal? A disposal? What's it got to do with?'

'No idea. Miss … Miss …'

'Coombe,' said Prunella.

'Miss Coombe wants to know. Not the daughter of the judge by any chance?'

'Yes, I'm afraid so.'

'Don't apologise. He's jolly good. My name's Dexter. Whose chambers are you in?'

'Harroway's.'

'You're lucky to get in there.'

'I'm still a pupil.'

'Oh, I see. My chambers are next door to yours as a matter of fact. Funny I haven't noticed you before.'

'I only came yesterday.'

'That explains it.'

'Pru,' intervened Jane, 'oughtn't you to find out what a disposal is?'

CHAPTER SIX

Miss Pringle's Will

Jane served her articles with Messrs Crestfall and Pusey, which was not simply a firm name but consisted of a Mr Crestfall and a Mr Pusey. Messrs Crestfall and Pusey made no attempt to rely on the past glories of solicitors long since dead or retired. They were satisfied with their own names. They had nearly all the qualities of the first-class solicitor. They were clean, civil personages of absolute integrity and high intelligence. They never exceeded the speed limit in their motorcars or left them (even outside the Law Society) where they could be calculated to cause an obstruction. Their offices were in Lincoln's Inn and, as soon as Prunella started to read as a pupil in the Temple, the girls were able to lunch together on most days.

One day, when Jane had been articled for three years, Mr Crestfall sent for her.

'Miss Coombe,' he said, 'I should like to send you on a rather delicate mission. There is a Miss Pringle, an elderly spinster, an old client of ours, who wants to make a will. Would you kindly go and take her preliminary instructions?'

'Wherein lies the delicacy, Mr Crestfall?' asked Jane. 'I have a feeling that she may want to make a considerable bequest to this firm.'

'How nice,' said Jane.

'It isn't nice at all,' said Mr Crestfall. 'In the first place, neither my partner nor I would like to take it. On the other hand we should hate to hurt the lady's feelings. But, if she insists on including us in the will, she will have to be separately advised. Now the difficulty is that she will refuse to be separately advised. I want you in effect to make a preliminary investigation. If you can steer her off making any bequest to us, that will be fine but, if not, see how strong her reactions are to the suggestion that she should take separate advice. When we know what the form is, we shall know best how to tackle the situation.'

Jane said that she would do her best and went to see Miss Pringle in Hampstead.

'You're not a solicitor, young woman,' said Miss Pringle.

'I'm an articled clerk.'

'Humph,' said Miss Pringle. 'I should have thought I was worth a partner. Anyway, I don't like to see women doing men's jobs. And it's worse if they're pretty like you are. How can a beautiful thing like you deal with the grimy, slimy things of the law?'

'I'm sure your will isn't grimy or slimy,' said Jane.

'That's all you know,' said Miss Pringle. 'I haven't washed myself for a week.'

Jane had not noticed any unpleasant sign of this as she came into the room, but almost automatically slightly shifted her chair.

'You needn't move away. I'm quite savoury. I've had someone to wash me. All over. Once a day. But I prefer to do it myself.'

'I'm sure you'll be able to in a day or two.'

'And why, may I ask? You did say you were an articled clerk, not a medical student, didn't you? I suppose we'll find doctors sending students to do their rounds for them soon. Don't see why they shouldn't, if solicitors send clerks. What d'you know about making wills?'

'Well,' said Jane, 'I once knew a solicitor who left two lines out of a will and someone lost a legacy by it.'

'Not Mr Crestfall, by any chance?'

'Oh, no – I'm sure he'd never do that.'

'You seem to be sure of a lot of things, young lady. You know when I'll be able to wash myself, and what mistakes Mr Crestfall won't make. How old are you, may I ask?'

'Twenty-three.'

'You ought to be a ballet dancer or something. What are you doing in a stuffy office? What's your father?'

'He's a judge, as a matter of fact.'

'I knew a judge once – Mr Justice Prendergast. A fine man. Only one thing against him. Couldn't stop twitching his ears. Horribly fascinating. Sometimes he'd move the one, sometimes the other and sometimes both together. And another thing too. His forehead used to go up and down. I suppose the wig went with it. Must have looked odd. Never saw him in Court. Used to play tennis together. Couldn't help watching his ears. Hit him with a service on the back of the head once. That made them twitch all right. What have you come to see me about? Oh, of course, my will. Why didn't Mr Crestfall come himself? Suppose he wanted to see what I was going to say first. Well, I'm not having any separate advice, that's flat. I'm not going to have any advice at all, if it comes to that. I know where I want to leave everything. I may not always be able to wash myself, but there's nothing wrong with my mind. Nothing, d'you hear? Do you notice anything wrong with it? Don't answer, you wouldn't say, if you did. I can see Mr Crestfall's face if you told him you'd told a client she was potty. Well, I'm not, see. Maybe one day, though. Then I shan't be able to make a will. Must be of sound mind, memory and understanding. That's right, isn't it?'

'Yes, I think so,' said Jane.

'Now there's a thing you ought to be sure of, young lady. That's the law. I, Felicia Pringle, being of sound mind, memory and understanding do make this my first will and testament.'

'Shouldn't it be last?' asked Jane.

'It isn't my last. It's my first.'

'All the forms say "last",' said Jane.

'They can say what they like. This is my first and I'm going to call it first. If I have another, we'll call it second.'

'In that way you'll never be able to put last. You'll never know if you're going to make another.'

'What's wrong with the truth? This is my first will, and I'm going to say so.'

'I suppose,' said Jane, 'they use the word "last" because only the last one will be valid. So, by the time it's proved, it is your last will.'

'Well, in that case, you can call this my first and last will. And you can call the next one my second and last will, and so on.'

'But then it'll turn out not to be true. If you make a second will your first won't be your last.'

'Well, that happens today, doesn't it? People are always changing wills and calling each of them their last.'

'Yes, and that's true.'

'Then we're back where we started. Anyway, this is my will and it's my first. So it's going to be called my first. Now, another thing. I'm not having that bit about revoking all other wills. I haven't made any, so I can't revoke them. It would be telling a lie, pretending I'd made other wills when I hadn't.'

'I think it only says "any" wills – that is any will you may have made. It doesn't say that you have made any.'

'But, if I haven't made any, I can't revoke any, can I?'

'I suppose not.'

'And anyway doesn't a second will automatically revoke previous wills?'

'Yes, I believe it does.'

'Then what's the point of saying so? D'you charge so much a line? No – my will begins like this: "This is my first will. I do not revoke any previous wills because there aren't any and anyway they'd be automatically revoked by this." That's how it's to begin. If you don't like it, send Mr Crestfall to see me. And if he doesn't like it, I'll see Mr Pusey. And if he doesn't like it, I'll do it just the same. After all, it's my will, not yours or Mr Crestfall's.'

'Very well, Miss Pringle. Now, what bequests do you wish to make?'

'None.'

'Then you leave everything to …?'

'No one. Take this down. I leave nothing to no one. I know the grammar's bad, but it has rather a pleasant sound about it. Nothing to no one. Your firm had better be my executors.'

'Then they'd get all the estate?'

'Well, what are you grumbling about?'

'But they're your solicitors.'

'Would you be here if they weren't?'

'But, Miss Pringle, if you leave all your money to your own solicitors, people might think they'd persuaded you to do so.'

'Why shouldn't they? There are worse people than Mr Crestfall and Mr Pusey. Much worse, I should say. Better too, no doubt, but I don't know them. I'm a recluse, girl, if you know what that is.'

'You prefer to be by yourself.'

'Have done for years. It isn't that I mind people so much – they're all right so long as they don't talk. It's then I can't stand them. "Good morning, Miss Pringle, and how are you this morning?" As if they cared. I know what they say about me behind my back. Potty. That's what they say. You'll do the same, I suppose.'

'Certainly not, Miss Pringle.'

'Why are you so certain? Most recluses are potty. Why shouldn't I be? It's our privilege. I nearly called this house Potty Corner. Do you read at all?'

'Yes,' said Jane, 'quite a lot.'

'I used to write books once.'

'So does my mother.'

'Worth reading?'

'Well, not really, but they pass the time.'

'Is that why *you* read?'

'Sometimes, on a journey.'

'My books were about gardens. They're not in print any longer.'

'You didn't write *Weeds are my Business*? I was brought up on it.'

'It was a bad book, but I enjoyed writing it. Not much use to anyone except myself. But you still have a copy?'

'Oh, yes. It's in the glass bookcase where we keep special books.'

'You wouldn't like to be one of my executors, I suppose?'

'That would be as bad as making Mr Crestfall or Mr Pusey. Can't you think of a friend or a relation?'

'And suppose I could? That's my business, isn't it?'

'Or some charity, perhaps?'

'There oughtn't to be any charities. The Royal Society for this and the National Society for that. These things ought to be done by the public as a whole, and if potty old men and women stopped leaving legacies to them they'd have to be.'

'What about some deserving person – an artist or an actor or an author who needs help to keep going?'

'What do you mean by "deserving"? People deserve what they get and get what they deserve. If you give an artist enough to live on he gets lazy.'

'Well, what about some old people who live on National Assistance?'

'If National Assistance isn't enough, I'm not going to go on encouraging the government to give too little. That's the same as the charities. If it is enough, there's no need.'

'The Church then.'

'The Church has gone into business. If it can afford to employ the Wells organisation it doesn't need my help.'

'Animals then?'

'Then they'd say I was potty. Left all her money to a cats' home. I know how they talk.'

'What about the Chancellor of the Exchequer?'

'He's been squeezing me for years and he'll extract the last ounce when I'm dead – no thank you. How much d'you think they'll assess the value of the film rights of *Weeds are my Business*?'

'What about one of the picture galleries, then? That would help to keep some good pictures in England.'

'That's for the nation to do. If the pictures are good enough for the nation to keep, the nation should buy them. If they're not, they should be left well alone.'

'What about sport? They can always do with some help.'

'What d'you mean by "sport"?'

'Oh – cricket, tennis, football …'

'D'you call that sport? No one kills anything.'

'Hunting, then?'

'If a hunt can't pay its own way, it ought to give up.'

'Research, perhaps?'

'Into what?'

'Anything – science, medicine, archaeology …'

'There's too much research. People are too inquisitive. What's it matter if the earth goes round the sun or the sun goes round the earth? Keats would have written his poems, Bach and Beethoven would have composed, Garrick would have acted either way. I don't actually mind people going off to Mars, if that's what they want to do, but there's plenty to see in their own world first. My money would have given out long before they'd seen everything here.'

'Nuclear weapons, then?'

'Yes, you have a point there. We've had enough wars. It's time for peace. Yes, I might leave my money for that. For two thousand years we've been preaching peace through love and a nice mess we've made of it. But peace through fear is better than no peace at all. And, as long as both sides have enough weapons to blow the other side's blooming heads off, they won't use them. At least there's a chance they mightn't. All right, that'll do. How are you going to word it?'

'Well, Mr Crestfall will have to consider that. But I suppose you could leave everything to trustees on trust to use the money for the creation of modern weapons for the preservation of peace of the world.'

'Is that what they'd describe as a charitable trust?'

'I'm not sure,' said Jane. 'As a matter of fact it's a little unusual.'

'Of course it's unusual – but so am I, aren't I? But not potty. Now run along, there's a good girl. I've talked as much as I can listen to.'

Jane went back to her employers.

'We will have to consult counsel about this. It might be void as against public policy, or be too vague. Make an appointment with Mr Creak. He's the man for this. He drafted the settlement in that nudist colony case. Most complicated.'

'Shall I write and ask Miss Pringle if she minds our instructing counsel?'

'On no account. It would involve us in interminable correspondence. We'll just do it, and, if she objects in the end, we'll pay the fees ourselves. But you're quite right to think of it. In most cases we'd ask permission first. As you've done so well with this matter perhaps you'd go and see Mr Creak and ask if he wants any further information.'

So Jane prepared the papers for Mr Creak who was indeed one of the finest draftsmen on the Chancery side. In due course he asked to see her and she attended a conference at his chambers in Lincoln's Inn.

As she was shown into his room Mr Creak was sitting at his desk with his head down, writing slowly. He looked up for a moment, but without any alteration of the blank expression on his face, and then returned to his papers. The clerk indicated to Jane that she should sit down and she did so. About a minute later Mr Creak suddenly stood up with a welcoming smile on his face.

'How d'you do? Please sit down.'

'How d'you do?' said Jane from where she sat.

'This will be Miss Pringle's will,' he said. 'Odd, very odd.'

He then returned to his papers and continued writing. Half an hour later he got up and extended a hand across the table. Jane got up and shook it.

'Thank you so much,' said Mr Creak. 'I think you've told me all I want. Most grateful. Goodbye,' and he indicated that the conference was over.

'The papers will be ready for you tomorrow,' said Mr Creak's clerk, as he showed her out.

'Can you tell me why Mr Creak wanted to see me?' Jane asked Mr Crestfall. 'He only said "Odd, very odd," apart from "how d'you do" and "goodbye".'

'That was unusually talkative for Mr Creak,' said Mr Crestfall. 'He must have liked you. No – he always wants someone to come to see him in case there are any points to raise. But, if the instructions are good, there seldom are. It's much better than Mr Stopforth, who goes on talking the whole time. You'll get used to the ways of counsel. Talking of which, we must try to find a little thing for your sister when she's called. If she's as good as you she'll do jolly well. Ask Mr Pocket if he's got a little County Court matter we can send her. She can't come to much harm with that.'

'What about the client, though?' asked Jane.

'Oh – he'll be all right. Mr Pocket won't take any chances. A judgment summons or something.'

And so it came about that Prunella was sent to deal with a 'disposal.' This means a case in which the plaintiff is entitled to judgment and the only question is how the defendant should pay or some matter of that kind, but, as it is unusual for counsel to attend on these occasions, few of them know what the term means.

CHAPTER SEVEN

Marking Time

Prunella's second case was not a brief of her own. Jane's firm had instructed a member of the chambers where Prunella was a pupil to appear in a County Court. Unfortunately, the barrister concerned, a Mr Waterhead, had a case in another court at the same time. He hoped to finish the other action in time to conduct the whole of the second case. But Prunella was sent to the Court to try to keep the case from coming on and, if it did come on, to try to keep the plaintiff in the witness box until Mr Waterhead arrived to cross-examine him.

For this purpose Prunella in the first instance had to try to persuade her opponent to allow the case to go to the bottom of the list. This meant that her opponent would have to spend the day in the County Court, instead of getting back at the luncheon adjournment. This was one of the few occasions where her looks served her in good stead. It was very difficult for Mr Dunham-Lewthwaite, who was not usually more co-operative with his colleagues than was absolutely necessary, to refuse Prunella's request. And, when it was backed up by an equally attractive Jane, he felt compelled to capitulate. At least, however, he was given the solace of a couple of hours' chat with two most attractive girls. But, at the end of that time, the judge had no more to do and the case was called on. Prunella did in fact ask Judge Groyne if he could possibly wait a few minutes more for what she called her learned leader to arrive, but even the attractions of Prunella could not persuade the judge to postpone the hearing of his last case. When it was over he could go home.

'No, I'm afraid, Miss Coombe, we shall have to begin. I am sure you will make a most efficient substitute for Mr Waterhead.'

It was Prunella's task to ask as many questions as possible but they had to be either irrelevant or only on the fringe of the case. Otherwise, when Mr Waterhead arrived and started to cross-examine on the important matters, it might be objected by his opponent or the judge that these matters had already been dealt with.

The case began. It was about a squabble between two neighbours. There were allegations and cross-allegations of assault and trespass. The trespass alleged by the plaintiff was the placing of a fence, the plaintiff said, one inch upon the plaintiff's land. The defendant, on the other hand, complained of a trespass by the plaintiff in removing the fence which, the defendant said, was entirely on his, the defendant's, land. The alleged assault took place while the plaintiff was removing the fence. Both parties were unreasonable, but it was important from Prunella's client's point of view that the judge should think that the plaintiff was the more unreasonable. Mr Waterhead was quite capable of cross-examining the plaintiff to good purpose. Prunella was not. She knew nothing of the art. So, somehow or other, she had to question the witness until Mr Waterhead arrived. Jane, of course, was there to back her up.

After Mr Dunham-Lewthwaite had opened his case, he called the plaintiff and examined him in chief. Then he sat down and Prunella, with her heart beating overtime, got up to cross-examine. At first she had an attack of stage-fright.

'Mr Haywell,' she said, and stuck at that.

'Ask him how old he is,' whispered Jane.

'How old are you?' asked Prunella, parrot-like.

'What on earth has that got to do with it?' interrupted Mr Dunham-Lewthwaite.

'It will transpire in due course,' whispered Jane.

Prunella repeated this.

'I'm afraid I'd like it to transpire now,' said the judge.

'If your Honour pleases,' said Prunella, and waited for it to transpire.

'We want to know what proportion of his life he's spent bickering with his neighbours and we can't know the proportion if we don't know how long his life has been,' whispered Jane.

'Really,' said the judge, after Prunella had enlightened him. 'It doesn't matter what the proportion is. If your case is that he's always quarrelling with his neighbours, put some of the quarrels to him.'

'Haven't you always quarrelled with your neighbours?' asked Prunella dutifully.

'Never,' said the plaintiff, 'except with this one, and a saint would quarrel with him.'

'What saint?' asked Prunella.

'Any saint.'

'Name a few.'

'Really,' said the judge, 'you can't ask that.'

'If your Honour pleases,' said Prunella, and turned to her sister for some more ammunition.

'Ask him if he hasn't had three different neighbours in the last five years, and didn't they all leave?'

The plaintiff said yes, they all left. He wished the defendant would too. Then they might have some peace.

'Why did your last neighbour leave?' asked Prunella at Jane's suggestion.

'Because he wanted to, I suppose.'

'Wasn't it because you made things intolerable for him?'

'Certainly not. We were very good friends – that is … until the trouble over the air-gun.'

'Follow up the air-gun,' whispered Jane. 'You should be able to take ten minutes over that one at least.'

'What air-gun?'

'D'you mean the make?'

'Yes, what make was it?'

'I don't know. It was just an air-gun.'

'Whose?'

'It belonged to the boy named Don.'

At this stage the patience of Mr Dunham-Lewthwaite began to give out – even though his opponents were two exceptionally pretty girls.

'Couldn't my learned friend start to deal with the facts of *this* case?' he said. 'We shall be here all night at this rate.'

'*You* may be,' said the judge, 'but *I* shan't.'

Half-an-hour later the twins – because it was certainly a joint effort – were still cross-examining the plaintiff about his neighbours – the ones on the other side.

'I do think,' said the judge, 'that it is about time you came to the matters in dispute between *these* parties, Miss Coombe.'

'I shall be coming to those, your Honour,' said Prunella.

'Some time next year,' said Mr Dunham-Lewthwaite.

'Ask him not to be offensive,' said Jane.

'Please don't be offensive,' said Prunella.

'Now, really,' said the judge, 'this bickering between counsel is most unsatisfactory.

'I'm sorry, your Honour,' said Mr Dunham-Lewthwaite, 'but my learned friend is wasting time and I'm getting tired of it.'

'Mr Dunham-Lewthwaite,' said the judge, 'you are a good deal senior to your learned opponent. Without in any way criticising her conduct of this case, I think a little latitude can be shown to practitioners of more recent call.'

'I am tempted to say,' replied Mr Dunham-Lewthwaite, 'that by the time this case is over, my learned opponent will have been called as long as I have been now.'

'You should resist the temptation then,' said the judge. 'And I should remind you that these discussions are merely prolonging the case. Shall we get on? Your next question, Miss Coombe, please.'

'What does your family consist of?' asked Prunella, prompted by her sister.

'He's already answered that,' said Mr Dunham-Lewthwaite.

'Not completely,' whispered Jane.

'Who is conducting this case?' said Mr Dunham-Lewthwaite angrily.

'Now, Mr Dunham-Lewthwaite, you mustn't get angry. A solicitor is entitled to instruct her counsel.'

'But she's asking all the questions, your Honour.'

'I can't hear that from here,' said the judge, 'and, if I could, she's quite entitled to suggest questions.'

'Suggest!' said Mr Dunham-Lewthwaite. 'She just repeats them like a parrot.'

'How dare you!' said Prunella.

'I shall rise for ten minutes to give you both an opportunity to recover your tempers,' said the judge, and rose.

'Well done, Pru,' said Jane. 'That was a master-stroke.'

Ten minutes later the case was resumed.

'I was asking you about your family,' said Prunella to the witness.

Mr Dunham-Lewthwaite swore quietly.

'Have you got a dog?'

'Yes.'

'Is it not treated as one of the family?'

'We're fond of dogs.'

'I dare say,' said Prunella. 'So are a lot of people. But isn't your dog treated as one of the family?'

'What's that got to do with the case?'

'His Honour will decide that,' said Prunella. 'Doesn't it sit up for its meals with the family *and* look at television?'

'Why shouldn't it? It likes it.'

'If anyone said anything about your dog that you didn't like, you'd resent it, wouldn't you, as much as if it were said about your wife or daughter?'

'If someone called your dog a dirty, snarling, pampered bitch, you'd resent it, wouldn't you?'

'You mustn't ask counsel questions,' said the judge, 'but at the moment I'm at a loss to see what all this has to do with the case.'

Mr Dunham-Lewthwaite could not resist interposing that it was as much to do with the case as anything else that Prunella had asked. It was an unwise move.

'Then you don't object?' said the judge.

'Of course I object,' said Mr Dunham-Lewthwaite, 'but it doesn't seem the slightest use.'

'That is a most improper remark,' said the judge. 'I shall rise for ten minutes until you can control yourself,' and he went and had another cigarette.

Half-an-hour later, while Prunella with Jane's help was still marking time, Mr Waterhead arrived.

'Thank God!' said Mr Dunham-Lewthwaite, caring not so much whether he won or lost the case as whether it would ever come to an end.

'What was that remark?' asked the judge, who was ready for another smoke.

'I said I was glad to see my learned friend,' said Mr Dunham-Lewthwaite.

'I see,' said the judge, and resisted the temptation to rise.

Within a few minutes Mr Waterhead was cross-examining the plaintiff about things that really mattered, and within half an hour he was chasing the unfortunate witness round the ring unmercifully. Even Mr Dunham-Lewthwaite began to prefer the irrelevancies of Prunella to the swift uppercuts and steady pounding which Mr Waterhead was delivering to the witness. There was no doubt whom the witness liked the better. Eventually he even said: 'Why should I be asked all these questions? The other one didn't.'

After a further half-hour of punishment the plaintiff asked if he could sit down. A quarter of an hour later he asked for a glass of water. Ten minutes later he capitulated.

'Well done,' said Mr Waterhead to Prunella, in the robing-room. 'How on earth did you keep it going for so long?'

'It was Jane, really,' said Prunella. 'I just did what she told me.'

'Well, between you it was a cracking job of work. If you hadn't kept him in the witness box till I came, we'd have lost that case. Our man would have been worse than he was. Jolly good. How did she do, George?' and he turned towards his opponent.

'I'll tell you on the way home,' said Mr Dunham-Lewthwaite grimly.

CHAPTER EIGHT

The Case of Mr Tewkesbury

Jane had been qualified three years before she briefed
Prunella in a High Court case. It was an action for
negligence against a solicitor, a Mr Tewkesbury. He was
not insured against such emergencies but he had
persuaded Jane, whom he had picked up when she slipped
down the stairs at the Law Society, to take on his case. He
was an elderly man and, in spite of the smell of stale
whisky which she couldn't help noticing even when she
was on the ground, she took quite a liking to him. Had
she been fully aware of his history it is doubtful if she
would have accepted his instructions but, by the time she
learned all about him, it was too late: and, as he did
nothing to justify her withdrawing from the case except to
drink more than would have been good for most people
but an amount which seemed entirely beneficial to him,
she felt she must see it through. Besides, she was now in
practice entirely on her own, with only a boy of sixteen to
help her, and clients were not as many as they might be.
But her father still made her and Prunella a small
allowance and they enjoyed playing about with the law.

Mr Tewkesbury's case was certainly one which lent itself
to such treatment.

'I put it to you that you were obviously drunk when you took my client's instructions,' said counsel.

Mr Tewkesbury affected to look pained. 'That I was obviously drunk?' he asked.

'Don't repeat the question, sir, kindly answer it.'

'If I was *obviously* drunk, why did he give me his instructions?'

'Don't ask me questions, sir, answer mine.'

Mr Tewkesbury thought for a moment.

'The best answer I can give you is that I was obviously not obviously drunk.'

'Were you drunk?'

'That's quite a different question.'

'Kindly answer it.'

'What exactly do you mean by drunk?'

'I mean drunk, sir. Unfit by reason of alcohol to conduct your affairs.'

'Then I was certainly not drunk, sir. I may have been *fit* by reason of alcohol to conduct my affairs. I won't deny that – but unfit, never.'

'The plaintiff says that he could smell your breath across the room.'

'I don't doubt it, sir. You may even be as lucky in this Court – though it's considerably larger. May I remind you, Mr Bone, that I am charged with negligence, not with having alcoholic breath. And I should like to add ...'

'Please don't,' said the judge, 'I take it that you are sober now?'

'As sober as I ever am, my Lord. I should not dream of coming into Court in any other condition.'

'In view of the fact that you were going to give evidence today, don't you think you might have refrained from alcohol until your evidence was concluded?' asked the judge.

'I consulted my doctor on that subject,' said Mr Tewkesbury. 'He said it would be most unwise. If I did that, he said, everything would appear unreal to me. As it is, I feel perfectly at home.'

'Don't make speeches, please, Mr Tewkesbury,' said the judge.

'I'm sorry, my Lord. I was trying to satisfy your Lordship as to my condition.'

'I'm quite satisfied about that,' said the judge.

'Thank you, my Lord,' said Mr Tewkesbury. 'Now, some more questions, please, Mr Bone,' he said, turning himself towards counsel.

Mr Bone tried to look unconcerned. He had at first tried to bully Mr Tewkesbury and then to ignore him. Neither course seemed very satisfactory. Mr Tewkesbury seemed to avoid his blows with ridiculous ease, while to ignore someone you are cross-examining is almost a contradiction in terms. Mr Bone decided he would adopt a third course and try to get on good terms with the witness.

'Now, Mr Tewkesbury,' he said, 'I'm sorry if we've been misunderstanding one another. I expect it was my fault.'

'I expect so,' said Mr Tewkesbury, 'but I'm quite used to that sort of thing.'

'Don't be impertinent to counsel, please,' said the judge.

'I'm sorry, my Lord,' said Mr Tewkesbury. 'I was trying to put him at his ease. Then we could get on a lot better.'

'You will kindly leave it to me to see how we get on,' said the judge curtly.

Mr Tewkesbury looked as apologetic as he could and, without raising either hand, gave the impression that he was finishing off a drink – to take away a nasty taste. It was impossible to commit him for contempt of Court, as he had done nothing except to open his mouth very slightly, give a faintly perceptible swallow and then close his mouth again.

'Come along, Mr Bone,' said the judge a trifle irritably. 'Is that all you wish to ask?'

'Indeed no, my Lord. I don't find this the easiest of witnesses.'

'If I can help in any way …' began Mr Tewkesbury.

'I'm sure you want to,' said Bone, continuing with his new line of approach.

'To be quite truthful, I don't,' said Mr Tewkesbury, 'but it's my duty to and so I will.'

'Very well, then. What questions did you ask my client at the first interview to see if he had a good cause of action?'

'May I look at my notes?'

'Certainly, if they were made at the time.'

'My solicitor has them.'

Jane handed some papers to the usher who handed them on to Mr Tewkesbury. He gazed at them for some little time.

'Is that what you want?' asked Mr Bone.

'It's what I've got,' said Mr Tewkesbury. 'I can't say that I particularly want them.'

'Mr Tewkesbury,' said the judge severely, 'if you are sober you must behave yourself. If you are drunk, it will be my painful duty to send you to prison.'

Mr Tewkesbury said nothing. After a short pause, the judge said: 'Well, which is it to be?'

'Sober, my Lord,' said Mr Tewkesbury.

'Very well, then, behave yourself. Are those the documents you want?'

Mr Tewkesbury said nothing, but looked towards Prunella for support. She looked at her sister. The judge repeated the question.

'What can I say, my Lord?' said Mr Tewkesbury. 'I've sworn to tell the truth. I don't want these or any other documents. I don't want to be here. But if I say so you'll say I'm not behaving myself.'

Jane whispered to Prunella – who stood up.

'Mr Tewkesbury,' she said, 'what his Lordship means is – are those the documents you need for the purpose of answering the question?'

Mr Tewkesbury smiled happily.

'Thank you very much, Miss Coombe,' he said. 'I'm sorry, my Lord.'

He then proceeded to look through the documents once more. As he did so his face clouded again.

'Can I speak to my counsel, do you think, my Lord?' he asked.

'In the middle of cross-examination? Certainly not,' said the judge. 'What's the difficulty?'

'My Lord,' said Mr Tewkesbury, 'I'm sorry to say we're back where we started. I neither want nor need these documents.'

'Do they not contain the entry for the date in question?'

'Yes, my Lord.'

'Then of course you need them. Do you mind if I ask him to read out what it says, Mr Bone?'

'I should be most grateful, my Lord.'

'Well, what does the entry for the 5th July say?'

'It's quite illegible, I'm afraid, my Lord. There's a word that looks like "pig," but I don't think it can be, as the plaintiff wasn't consulting me about pigs. And there's another word that looks like "stinkers," but he wasn't consulting me about them either. Oh – but perhaps he was referring to the tenants down below.'

'Now we're getting somewhere, Mr Tewkesbury,' said Mr Bone still affably. 'My client wanted to know if he could get his tenants out. That was it, wasn't it?'

'Certainly,' said Mr Tewkesbury, 'but I could have told you that from my bill of costs. That's typed. Indeed, here it is. "To advising you about the tenants downstairs." Two guineas. Not unreasonable, I think.'

'But the point is, Mr Tewkesbury, what did you advise my client? He wanted to know if he'd succeed in an action for possession against his tenant. What did you tell him?'

'I expect I said – try it and see.'

'Without going into the question whether he had any legal right to evict the tenant?'

'Well, it wouldn't have made any difference if I had. He lost the case.'

'That's his complaint, Mr Tewkesbury. He says that you let him bring an action which he had no chance of winning.'

'He had a very good chance, sir,' said Mr Tewkesbury. 'Some of the most likely looking cases are lost, sir, and some of the most unlikely won, sir. It's a toss up. This case of mine, for instance, will I win it or lose it?'

'You will go to prison before either event,' said the judge, 'if you don't behave yourself. I've had just about enough of your client's antics, Miss Coombe. Perhaps you'd better have a word with him. I shan't give him another chance.'

'Thank you, my Lord,' said Prunella. 'I'll get my solicitor to speak to him.'

'Very well,' said the judge. 'I'll rise for five minutes to give you the opportunity.'

'I'm very much obliged, my Lord.'

As soon as the judge had risen, Jane went to Mr Tewkesbury in the witness box and held a whispered conversation with him.

'How's it going, d'you think?' he said, as Jane approached him. 'I must say your sister looks beautiful in her robes. But then you'd look the same. I couldn't tell you apart, I swear I couldn't. How lucky you fell down those stairs.'

'Mr Tewkesbury,' said Jane, 'much as my sister and I like you, we shall withdraw from the case if you don't pull yourself together. You're driving the judge mad, and you'll not only lose but go to prison and be reported to the Law Society.'

'That's a lot for one day,' said Mr Tewkesbury. 'Why not settle the case instead?'

'We've tried to, but they want the full amount.'

'Well they'd better have it, hadn't they? If they're going to win anyway it's easier to pay them if I'm not in prison, isn't it. I'll tell you what – offer them solicitor and client costs if they'll withdraw the allegations of negligence.'

'D'you mean that?'

'Of course I do, my dear young lady. I believe I only fought the action to see you and your sister at work. And a very pretty sight too. Off with you now: go and talk to them before the judge comes back and eats me.'

Ten minutes later Mr Bone announced to the surprised judge that he was happy to say that his Lordship would no longer be troubled by the case. The parties had come to terms and all he need add was that the plaintiff withdrew all allegations against the defendant.

Mr Tewkesbury unsuccessfully offered to celebrate the occasion with Prunella and Jane, and eventually went off to do so by himself.

'As I told you, my dear girls,' he said, as he left, '*Potior est conditio defendentis* – which, in case you didn't know it, means in my case that the defendant enjoys better spirits.'

CHAPTER NINE

A Friendly Loan

It was not long after the case of Mr Tewkesbury that Prunella had met Digby Buttonstep and it was some six months after their meeting that the fateful dinner took place when the major showed how distressed he would be if his sons married Jane and Prunella.

About a month later Digby was in the Buttonstep Arms when a newcomer to the village got into conversation with him. They had a couple of drinks together and, after the second, the newcomer said that his name was Trotter and that he'd rented a small house near the Common. Did Digby by any chance know of some kind person who would lend him a motor mower for a day? Digby promised to ask his father.

The same evening he did so.

'Who is the chap?' asked his father. 'Not a lawyer, I hope.'

'Oh, no. He's in some kind of business. I met him at the local. Didn't seem a bad chap and we got talking.'

'All right,' said the major. 'But I must have it back by Friday.'

'I'll tell him,' said Digby, and the motor mower was lent to Mr Trotter.

Friday came and it was not returned. When Digby got home in the evening his father was not pleased.

'What about the mower? He hasn't brought it back.'

'I'm so sorry, father. I'll pop down and see him.'

'Might as well wait till the morning now. Can't use it till then. But it's too bad of the fellow.'

'I'll go first thing.'

Next morning Digby went out before breakfast. As soon as he came back, he told his father that the mower would be returned that morning.

'He says he's terribly sorry. He just forgot it. He'll bring it up by eleven.'

'Well, that's better than making excuses,' said the major. 'Thanks for going down so early.'

But when Digby came home that evening the mower had still not been returned.

'Look here,' said the major, 'It really is too bad. He can't have forgotten it again.'

'I'll go down after dinner. I really am most awfully sorry. It's my fault. I should never have asked you to lend it to him.'

'Oh, that's all right,' said the major. 'The world is made up of two sorts of people – reliable, and the other kind. You couldn't tell which kind he was over a couple of drinks. Who paid for them as a matter of interest?'

'I forget, as a matter of fact.'

'Humph,' said the major, 'I strongly suspect you paid for them both. Kindly tell the fellow from me that that mower is to be here first thing tomorrow morning.'

'Of course, father.'

Later that evening Digby returned from his errand with unsatisfactory news.

'He says he's got mumps in the house.'

'What on earth has that got to do with the mower?'

'Well, he's not feeling too good himself and doesn't think he ought to go out, and he wouldn't let me into the house as I'd never had them.'

'This is past a joke,' said the major. 'I'll go and see the fellow myself. Where does he live?'

'He's got that little house just before the common.'

'What's his name?'

'Trotter.'

'Right. Mumps or no mumps, that mower's coming back in the morning.'

'Are you sure it's wise, dear,' asked his wife. 'After all, if you've never had them and you go in the house you may get them.'

'Haven't they a back door or something?'

'That's the unfortunate thing. You have to go through the house.'

'But he can put it in the front garden and we can take it away.'

'I suggested that – but he said he really didn't feel strong enough to get it through the house.'

'Confound the man,' said the major. 'Not strong enough! What's his telephone number?'

'I don't know, but we can get it from the exchange.'

'Is that Mr Trotter,' asked the major a few minutes later.

'It is,' said a rather weak voice.

'This is Claude Buttonstep here. Would you be kind enough to put my mower in your front garden tomorrow morning, and I'll come and fetch it.'

'I'm so sorry to put you to all that trouble.'

'Tomorrow morning, then?'

'Very well,' said the faint voice. 'I'm so grateful for the loan.'

'Pah!' said the major, as he rang off.

The next morning he walked quickly to Mr Trotter's house. The mower was not in the front garden. The major knocked on the door. There was no answer. He knocked louder, but with no better result. Then he noticed there was a bell. He had rung it three times and knocked long and loudly before he gave it up. He went straight home and telephoned.

'Is that Mr Trotter?'

'It is,' said a faint voice.

'Why didn't you answer the door? I knocked and rang I don't know how many times.'

'I know. It kept me awake.'

'Look here, sir, why was my mower not in the front garden?'

'I didn't feel up to it, I'm afraid.'

'Have you no one else in the house?'

'No one who could move it, I'm afraid.'

'When am I going to get it back?'

'I'm terribly sorry about it.'

'I dare say, but when am I going to get it back?'

'Well – I'm most awfully sorry – you may have to wait till I get over my mumps.'

'The doctor says you've got them, does he?'

'I'm afraid I don't go in for doctors. They've killed too many of the family already. If you'll take my advice, you'll steer clear of them too.'

For once the major lost his temper although no lawyers were concerned.

'When I want your advice, I'll ask for it, sir. What I want at the moment is not *your* advice but *my* mower.'

'It is a problem, isn't it?' said Mr Trotter faintly.

'If you haven't had a doctor, how d'you know you've got mumps?'

'I've got a book.'

'I dare say you have. So have I.'

'Is yours by …?'

'Look here, sir,' broke in the major. 'I don't care whether you've got mumps or not. I want my mower back.'

'I know you do. I should feel exactly the same in your position. And, if you had mumps, you'd feel like me.'

'Are you going to return the machine, or not?'

'Of course I am, and I'm terribly sorry for the delay. But we seem to have reached an impasse.'

'When will you be better?'

'According to this book, I shall be ill for about a fortnight, and infectious for another fortnight after that. That means a month, doesn't it. Will you be able to manage till then? Perhaps you could borrow one from a friend?'

'What is to stop you putting the mower in the front garden when you feel better?'

'Oh, nothing – except that I'd prefer to return it to your house. It seems very ungrateful letting you fetch it. It's been so useful to me. And it's a jolly good machine. Except for the broken blade, of course.'

'The broken blade!' yelled the major. 'There was no broken blade when the machine was lent to you.'

'You mean that you think I've broken it?'

'I do.'

'I can hardly think so.'

'It was in perfect order when I lent it to you.'

'Well, so it is now – except, of course, just for the blade.'

'There was no broken blade when I lent it to you.'

'Have you any witnesses?'

The major slammed down the telephone. If he had said more he would have broken into language of which the local exchange – Mrs Temperley – would have disapproved, and he suspected that she had heard the whole conversation.

'What can I do with the fellow?' the major complained to his wife. 'He's obviously mad. Now he's broken the thing. Heaven knows what damage he's done. Why on earth did I ever let Digby persuade me to lend it to him?'

'Perhaps he could throw a key down and you could go through and fetch it. Or Archie could give you a hand.'

'Good idea. Thanks, darling.'

The major got on the telephone again and made the suggestion.

'I'm afraid it can't be done,' replied Mr Trotter.

'Why not?'

'Well, first of all I have to keep the windows closed. The book says so. And secondly, if you came through the house, you might pick up mumps and if you did, I'd never forgive myself.'

'Somebody else in the house can surely open the door to me, and I'll take the risk of that,' said the major grimly.

'Too dangerous. They've all got it now. Really I should borrow another, if I were you. And, as I told you, it's not working. So it wouldn't be much good to you if you did get it. And now, if you'll forgive me, I must go to sleep again. The book is most insistent on it.'

'Mr Trotter,' said the major, 'I've had enough of this. Unless the mower is delivered back here by noon tomorrow you will hear from my …'

Good heavens, he said to himself, I nearly said 'my solicitors.' He only just stopped in time.

'You will hear …' he repeated, but could not think how to go on.

'From whom shall I hear,' asked Mr Trotter politely, 'if the mower is not returned by noon tomorrow?'

81

'Oh, go to blazes,' said the major, and once again replaced the receiver in a fury. He had more reason to be angry now. He was almost as angry with himself for what he had nearly said as with Mr Trotter.

When Digby came home that evening, the major told him what had happened.

'But I saw him going into his house as I came along,' said Digby.

'Are you sure?' asked the major.

'Of course. If I'd known what had happened I'd have stopped him going in. But naturally I thought you'd had the machine back, and it's all been rather embarrassing – so I didn't particularly want to speak to him.'

The major telephoned Mr Trotter.

'My son tells me he's seen you outside your house.'

'I didn't see him.'

'He saw you.'

'Very likely. I took a stroll.'

'Then why haven't you put out the machine?'

'I didn't feel up to it. It's too heavy.'

'And what were you doing out, if you've got mumps?'

'Well, as a matter of fact the book says …'

'Confound the book. Will you kindly leave your front door open and my son and I will come and fetch the mower.'

'I'm afraid I couldn't agree to that.'

'You what!?'

'I'm in bed, you see. I couldn't risk going to the door. Perhaps in the morning. But I really don't know why you're so anxious about it. You can't use the thing. I'm not sure that two blades haven't gone.'

The major replaced the receiver.

'D'you know, Digby, I don't believe he ever intends to give up the mower. I shall go to see old Glossop in the morning.'

So in the morning, before he went on his rounds, PC Glossop received a call from the major.

'What can I do for you, sir?'

'Have you had the mumps, Glossop?'

'Mumps, sir? Well I have, as a matter of fact,' said the constable, showing surprise in his voice.

'Good,' said the major. 'I want you to arrest a man for stealing. He says he's got mumps, but I don't believe it.'

'What's the charge, sir?'

'Stealing my motor mower.'

'When did he take it, sir?'

'I lent it to him and he won't give it back.'

'That's not stealing I'm afraid, sir – not if you lent it to him. If he's made away with it, it might be what the lawyers call fraudulent conversion.'

'Never mind about the lawyers. Can you get my mower back for me?'

'Well, I can ask him for it, sir, but I suppose you've done that?'

'I have indeed.'

'Why won't he give it back, sir?'

'He makes all sorts of excuses, but the truth is that the fellow's nuts, I suppose.'

'What does the doctor say, sir?'

'He won't have a doctor. He uses a book.'

'A book, sir?'

'Never mind. What can you do to get the thing back for me?'

'Well, we can go along together, sir, and try peaceful persuasion. But fraudulent conversion isn't really in my line. I'd have to get on to Copplestone about that. And I expect they'd be on to the super about it. It doesn't often come our way round here. Shall we go along, sir? I'll just put my coat on, sir.'

So the major and PC Glossop called on Mr Trotter's house. They rang and knocked, but nothing happened.

'He's in there all right, but he just won't answer.'

'Is there anyone in?' shouted the constable. He repeated the question loudly several times, but with no result.

'We'd best go back to my house and telephone,' said the major in the end.

Five minutes later PC Glossop was on the telephone.

'Is that Mr Trotter?'

'It is.'

'This is police-constable Glossop, sir. I've had a complaint from Major Buttonstep that he had lent you a motor mower and you won't give it back to him.'

'Won't give it back to him, constable? There must be some mistake. I want to give it back to him. It's no use to me and it's taking up room in the shed which I can ill spare.'

'We've just been to your house and couldn't get any reply.'

'I'm sorry, but I've got rather a cold and gone to bed.'

'Have you got mumps, sir?'

'Mumps? What on earth d'you mean? Nothing of the kind. I've got a cold.'

'The major tells me you said you had mumps and gave that as an excuse for not giving up the machine.'

'He must have misunderstood – this line is rather bad.'

'Well, would you kindly put the mower in your front garden, sir?'

'Not at the moment, I'm afraid. I don't feel up to it.'

'Then will you let me come and fetch it, sir?'

'No – I'm afraid not. It's not convenient. Tell the major to borrow one that works. Ask him to be kind enough to send for this one in the morning. Not before 10 or after 11. Goodbye, officer.'

'Well, sir,' said the constable, 'would you like me to come with you in the morning?'

'That's very good of you,' said the major. 'I think it might be a good idea. We might take the doctor too.'

But, in the end, only the major and PC Glossop attended at precisely 10.15 in the morning. No mowing machine was in the front garden. They rang and knocked and shouted, but to no effect.

'Can't we break the door down?' asked the major.

' 'Fraid not, sir. Forcible entry on land.'

'What about forcible detention of my property?'

'That's different, sir. I had a word with Copplestone as a matter of fact, sir, this morning. They say that, if he hasn't made away with it, it's nothing to do with the criminal law. If he has made away with it then, as I told you, it's what they call fraudulent conversion and we could summon him or get a warrant for his arrest. But you can't prove he's sold it or anything like that, can you, sir?'

'Of course I can't. But I can prove he's had it and won't give it back. Mr Trotter,' he shouted, but the answer was as before – silence. The major thundered on the door, but again with no result.

'D'you mean to say there's nothing you can do, Glossop? It's ridiculous.'

'Very sorry, sir, but, unless you can show he's made away with it, it isn't a police matter.'

'But you must be able to do something. There must be some law against it.'

'Oh, yes, sir. You could sue him in the County Court.'

'The County Court!' said the major. 'Never. I've had one go there, thank you. Cost me £50. The machine isn't worth that. Isn't worth anything I expect by now if he's smashed all the blades.'

'I'm no lawyer, sir, but if he's damaged it I expect you can make him pay for it.'

'How?'

'In the County Court.'

'The County Court!' the major almost howled. 'It'll probably cost me another fifty pounds to get no damages. No, thank you. Let's go and telephone the fellow again.'

They went back to PC Glossop's house and rang Mr Trotter's number.

'Daniel Trotter speaking.'

'This is Constable Glossop speaking, sir. I called round with the major to get the machine but it wasn't there and you wouldn't answer the door.'

'I thought you'd break it down. Mustn't do that, you know.'

'Why wasn't the machine there, sir?'

'Why? Because you came at the wrong time.'

'You said not before 10 or after 11, and we came at 10.15.'

'You must have misunderstood. I said before 10 or after 11.'

PC Glossop reported the conversation to the major.

'Well, it's after 11 now. Tell him we'll come for it right away.'

The constable made the suggestion.

'I'm afraid not, officer. When I heard you go away I thought you'd finished for the day and made my arrangements accordingly.'

'Let me speak to him,' said the major, who had heard Mr Trotter's last answer.

'Now, look here,' said the major, 'I don't know what your game is – whether you're mad or whether you've simply sold the machine – but I give you a final warning. Unless you put that machine out at once you will take the consequences.'

'Really,' said Mr Trotter. 'What a fuss to make about an old mower. And you mustn't suggest I'm mad, or that I've stolen your machine either. That's what most people call libel but lawyers call it slander. As you're standing next to the constable, he could hear what you said and I shall require an immediate apology or you will hear from my solicitors. You will have your machine back as soon as I've finished with it, and not before. After all, you lent it to me. If you didn't intend me to use it, why let me have it? That's what lawyers would call an implied condition.'

'I lent it to you for one day.'

'One day wasn't enough.'

'You promised to let me have it back on Friday.'

'Well, today's only Monday. Why get so hot under the collar? What's a couple of days? That's what lawyers would call *de minimis*.'

'Are you going to put that machine out in the front garden?'

'Certainly.'

'At once?'

'Not so certainly. In a day or two. Come back Thursday week. Or thereabouts. Oh, you'll be pleased to hear the blades aren't broken. It's going very well indeed – well, for an old machine it is.'

'That machine was bought new in June.'

'Well, it's a matter of use, isn't it? Some cars are almost as good as new after eighteen months: others have their gears ruined in three. Perhaps I could give you some lessons in how to use it. It's really had a caning, I must say.'

'How dare you, sir!' yelled the major.

'I haven't had that apology yet,' said Mr Trotter. 'Will you kindly say in an audible voice to the officer, so that I can hear it, that I am neither mad nor a thief.'

The major said nothing.

'I'm waiting,' said Mr Trotter.

'I will say nothing of the kind. You *are* one or the other.'

'I don't want the damages for myself,' said Mr Trotter, 'but you're certainly piling them up. That's twice you've said it now. The first time you only said it by what lawyers would call an innuendo. But this time you've said it directly. You said quite plainly that I was either mad or a thief.'

'And you are,' said the major. The continued reference to lawyers was making him frantic.

'Three times lucky,' said Mr Trotter. 'You've no idea what this is going to cost you. I shall give the money to a charity, of course. But you'd be able to buy half-a-dozen mowing machines with it. You see, I'm new in the village and you couldn't find a much more important person to slander me to than the village constable. If somebody steals something – a mowing machine for example – and they don't know who's done it, he'll suspect me because you say I've stolen yours. And if some madman sets fire to a hayrick, he'll suspect me because you say I'm mad. Oh, I know you only said I was mad *or* a thief, but that won't help you. That's what lawyers call a pregnant alternative.'

'Confound you, sir,' said the major, and replaced the receiver.

'I'm very sorry, sir,' said PC Glossop. 'He seems a very odd gentleman. What are you going to do, sir? County Court him?'

'Certainly not. I'm going to get back my machine, but not that way, thank you.'

Two nights later, while PC Glossop was on his nightly round, he saw a figure apparently trying to break into Mr Trotter's house.

'Who's that?' he said sternly.

'Sh – ' said the major.

The constable was now in an embarrassing situation. Major Buttonstep was one of the most respected residents and always to be relied upon for help for any of the village causes. PC Glossop was part of the village and liked and respected the major. He sympathised with him too. Mr Trotter had admittedly treated him very badly. But what was he, PC Glossop, to do? Turn a blind eye, or not? If anyone was awake in the house his voice might well have been recognised and he might be reported for a serious failure of duty. It wasn't burglary to break into a house to get back your own property, but it was certainly illegal and against the peace of our Lady the Queen. Should he cycle on, or give the major a leg up? His instincts were to do one or the other, but his sense of duty (and fears for his pension) rightly prevented him. He went over to the major and spoke softly: 'I'm afraid you can't do that, sir.'

'I'm doing it.'

'But it's unlawful to break into an inhabited house.'

'Isn't it unlawful to detain someone else's property?'

'Two wrongs don't make a right, sir. And if you break in, sir, it's a crime.'

'But it isn't a crime for him to keep my machine?'

'Not if it's only temporary.'

'The law's a bigger ass than even I thought.'

'Well, sir,' explained the constable who, while sympathising with the major, had a certain respect for the law and did not like to hear it too much abused, 'it's like this. If people were allowed to break into other people's houses, the result might be serious injury to one side or the other or both, sir. People will defend their houses, sir.'

'I'm only trying to defend my mowing machine.'

'Not defend, sir. Retake. Now, *peaceable* recapture of chattels, as the lawyers call it …'

But the major broke in. 'You and Mr Trotter are as bad as each other. I don't want to know what the lawyers call anything. I know what I call them.'

'Well, I'm very sorry, sir, but, while peaceable recapture of chattels is allowed – breaking into someone's inhabited house to get them isn't what the law calls peaceable. It might occasion a breach of the peace.'

'Go away,' said the major. 'You'll wake up everyone in the house.'

'You have,' said Mr Trotter, opening a window. 'Lock him up, please, officer. We'll deal with him in the morning.'

There was nothing for it. The major slid down the wall where he had been uncomfortably perched during the conversation.

'Burglars in Buttonstep,' said Mr Trotter. 'I wouldn't have believed it. 'Who is it?'

'It's me,' said the major angrily. 'I want my machine back.'

'What a silly time to come for it. You must be mixing it up with one of your military night-into-day exercises. But you're not in the Army now, major. Can't have been for a long time, I should imagine. Good night, officer. I shan't prefer any charge. But tell him not to do it again, will you? You really must behave yourself you know,' he added, directing his voice towards the major. 'Good night.' And he closed the window.

The major walked away with the constable.

'This is ludicrous, Glossop. What am I to do?'

'You could send him a solicitor's letter, sir,' said the constable, not very happily.

'I am not going to lawyers,' said the major.

'You could sue him in the County Court yourself – appear in person, I mean.'

'I'm not going to the County Court. Once in a lifetime is enough.'

'Well, sir, I'm afraid there isn't anything else I can suggest. As long as he's got the machine and is simply holding on to it too long it isn't a criminal matter. You can't retake it yourself, because it would involve forcible entry on to land – and that's been forbidden since the days of the first Queen Elizabeth.'

'D'you mean to say an old law like that is still in force? Bit long in the tooth, isn't it?'

'I suppose it is, sir, but they still use it. Well, sir, if you're not able to use the criminal law or to take it back peaceably yourself, the only alternative is to use the civil law and sue him.'

'Hell!' said the major. 'Well, thank you, Glossop. I'll speak to my son about it in the morning.'

The next morning at breakfast the major told Digby what had happened.

'It's outrageous, father. I'm terribly sorry about it. Why on earth didn't I realise that the fellow was a madman? What can we do? I'll go and see him myself as soon as I've finished breakfast.'

'I don't suppose he'll listen to you any more than he would to me.'

'It's worth trying, father. After all, I was the person he first asked for it. I'll go now, and I'll let you know what happens.'

Digby went down to Mr Trotter's house and rang the bell.

Mr Trotter put his head out of the window.

'Ah – good morning. I wonder if by any chance your father could lend me a roller. Just for a day, you know.'

'Mr Trotter,' said Digby, 'I should be most grateful if you'd let me have my father's mowing machine back first. Then we could discuss the roller.'

Digby spoke in the friendly and quiet manner most sensible people would use towards a lunatic.

'But I want to use one after the other,' said Mr Trotter.

'Haven't you finished with the mower yet?'

'I'm afraid not. Roll first and cut afterwards.'

'Isn't it the other way round?'

'Not here. Be a good chap and bring it round, would you?'

'I'm very sorry,' said Digby, 'I'm afraid my father wouldn't consider lending you the roller until you've handed back the mower.'

'How unfriendly. Are all the people in this village like your father?'

'Well, Mr Trotter, after all, he did lend the mower to you without knowing you. A lot of people wouldn't do that.'

'I don't see why not. It's not the sort of thing one can make away with easily.'

'No, but he couldn't tell how you'd use it and he might have wanted to use it himself. As a matter of fact he does.'

'Well, we can't both use it at the same time, can we?' By now a few of the villagers were standing around listening to the conversation.

'Mr Trotter,' said Digby rather more firmly, 'I really must ask you to bring the machine outside.'

'Why must you do that?'

'Because it's my father's machine and he wants it.'

'How badly does he want it?'

'Very badly, as a matter of fact.'

'Then why doesn't he come for it himself? Why bother you?'

'He's come several times, Mr Trotter, and you've refused to give it to him. That's why I offered to come this time.'

'He's certainly been here, bellowing like a bull, but I couldn't make head or tail of what he wanted. He brought a policeman with him once. What's he frightened of? Think I'll attack him or something? I shouldn't dream of attacking someone who's been good enough to lend me his mower.'

As they were talking, Digby saw the doctor's car approaching. He left Mr Trotter and went quickly into the road and stopped the car.

'Sorry to worry you, doctor, but would you mind coming to listen to this conversation? This fellow wants certifying, I think.'

The doctor got out of the car and walked back with Digby to the house.

'Mr Trotter,' said Digby, 'this is Dr Martin.'

'How d'you do, doctor?' said Mr Trotter. 'I'm new here. Hope I shan't be requiring your services for some time.'

'I hope not,' said the doctor.

'Mr Trotter,' said Digby, 'would you mind explaining to the doctor why you won't return father's mowing machine?'

'Well, I will,' said Mr Trotter, 'but last night your father tried to break into my house and I must confess I wasn't pleased.'

The doctor became interested. The idea of Major Buttonstep burgling somebody's house was ridiculous. Hallucinations obviously. Persecution mania probably. Tell by his face. Typical paranoic.

'But why didn't you let him have it back before then?' asked Digby.

'D'you mean to say,' said the doctor in a surprised voice, 'that your father *did* try to break in here? I can't believe it.'

'Well, he did as a matter of fact. I can explain.'

'Is your father all right?' asked the doctor, in an undertone. 'Perhaps I'd better come and have a look at *him*.'

'The only reason my father came here last night was because you'd refused time and again to give it back,' said Digby to Mr Trotter.

'I've never refused. It just wasn't convenient to let him have it back at the times he called. And I must say he wasn't very polite when he did come. He thundered on the door, and shouted, and he told the policeman I was either mad or a thief. And all because I was a trifle late in returning his machine. And then he tries to break into the house. It would have served him right if he'd broken in and I'd hit him on the head in mistake for a burglar. Come to think of it, from the way he's behaving perhaps someone has hit him on the head. No, after the way he's treated me I'm going to keep the machine for a few more days. Just to teach him a lesson. He'll get it back all right, but he must learn manners first. Now, if you'll forgive me, there are one or two things I've got to do.'

Mr Trotter closed the window.

'Well?' said Digby to the doctor.

'He seems sane enough to me,' said the doctor, 'but I must say it seems odd of your father to behave like that.'

'But you don't know what's happened,' said Digby. 'He's treated father outrageously.'

'Well, of course, if you say so, Digby, no doubt he has. But I can't see the slightest evidence of insanity. I did at first, when he spoke of your father trying to break in. I thought it must have been an hallucination. Well – see you again soon – I must be off.'

The doctor drove away, and Digby returned home and told the family what had happened.

'I'll have a go,' said John.

'It won't be any good,' said Digby.

'Well, something's got to be done,' said John, 'and I'm going down to see for myself what it's all about.'

Mr Trotter opened the window as soon as John had rung the bell.

'My name is John Buttonstep,' said John.

'Mine's Daniel Trotter,' said Mr Trotter. 'How d'you do?'

'I've come about the mowing machine.'

'I see,' said Mr Trotter. 'Are there any more of you?'

'My father would like his machine back, please.'

'But do tell me,' persisted Mr Trotter, 'have you any brothers and sisters?'

'Only the one you've seen.'

'Your mother still alive?'

'Yes.'

'She'll be coming later, I suppose?'

'No, she won't,' said John. 'I've come to warn you that, unless you give me the mower now, other steps will be taken to get it.'

'Other steps? Like breaking and entering, d'you mean? Because, if you do, I ought to warn you that I shan't be as nice about it next time. I told the policeman I wouldn't prefer a charge against your father last night. But if he or you or anyone tries it again I will. Good morning to you.'

Mr Trotter closed the window and John returned home to report the fruitless interview.

'Where do we go from here,' said Major Buttonstep. 'I'm hanged if I'll let the fellow get away with it. What d'you think, dear?'

'The same as you, darling,' said his wife. 'What an unpleasant man he must be.'

'Glossop says the only thing to do is to County Court him,' said the major. 'I can't bear the idea but, on the other hand, I'm not going to let him play fast and loose with me like this. I'll have to go to a solicitor, I suppose.' He shuddered at the idea.

'Shall I telephone old Dealtry?' suggested Digby.

'That old fool! Good heavens, no,' said the major. 'I expect they're all alike really, though. One's as bad as the other. But this fellow Trotter's worse.'

'Why not try Jane?' suggested John.

'Who's he?'

'Jane Coombe – the girl who came to dinner.'

'Is she really qualified?'

'Good Lord, yes, and she's jolly good I believe.'

'None of them is jolly good,' said the major, 'but she's certainly an attractive girl. And, if I've got to have a solicitor, I might as well have her. She charges the earth, I suppose? I'll show you some of the bills of costs we've had in the family.'

'I'm sure she wouldn't overcharge, father. Why not go and see her?'

The major hesitated, but, for the moment, his dislike of Mr Trotter exceeded his dislike of the law.

'All right,' he said, 'I'll go.'

CHAPTER TEN

First Blood

A few days later the major attended his first interview with a solicitor since his case with the chauffeur.

At first he found it quite agreeable, and he had to admit to himself that talking to a pretty girl was a much more pleasant way of consulting a lawyer than he had envisaged. But before very long trouble emerged. Jane was proposing to write a letter demanding the return of the mowing machine at once. The major wanted it to be returned to his house, but Jane was not altogether happy about that.

'You see,' she said, 'if no demand had been made before we wrote this letter, we should have to call on him at his house to demand it. I don't think he was under any legal obligation to bring it to your house. He may have been, but I doubt it.'

'Heavens alive, Miss Coombe!' said the major, 'what are lawyers for? Surely you know that quite definitely? It's the old case of the chauffeur all over again.'

'The point is, Major Buttonstep, that one wants to avoid any unnecessary risks, or having any technical points taken against us.'

'Technical points!' said the major. 'I lent him my mowing machine, and he won't give it back. What's technical about that?'

'It may seem very silly to you,' said Jane, 'but the position is this. An action for the return of goods cannot succeed unless there has been a demand and refusal ...'

'There have been a dozen demands and refusals.'

'I quite follow that,' said Jane, 'but, if there hadn't been ... '

'There *have* been, my dear girl. Forgive me talking to you like this, but really I don't know which is worse – talking to Mr Trotter or talking to a lawyer.'

'If you'd just let me finish,' went on Jane, 'what I wanted to say was this. If there had been no demand and refusal before we wrote, it would have been much too dangerous to tell him to bring it to your house. He could then have said that he had never refused to hand it over to you – but only failed to deliver it to your house, and that he was under no obligation to do that. In those circumstances an action for detinue, as we call it ...'

'Why call it that? It's all part of the abracadabra, I suppose, just so that no one else can understand.'

'Well, Major Buttonstep, my uncle was in the Army, and, if I may say so, there were a good many terms that the ordinary civilian wouldn't understand. ADOS, DADOS and so on.'

'You may have something there,' conceded the major, 'but at any rate they stand for English words. They aren't in this bastard Latin. Detinue – what on earth does it mean?'

'Detention of goods.'

'Then why not say so?'

'Well, detinue is shorter.'

'I've not noticed lawyers trying to do things the shortest way in my experience of them. They normally use six words where one would do.'

'As I was saying,' Jane went on, 'if the only demand was a letter calling for a return of the machine to your house, the action would probably fail. In fact, however, as you say, there have been plenty of demands at his house, so legally you don't need to write a letter at all. Your action for detinue would succeed if we simply issued a summons without writing a letter first.'

'Then why not do so?'

'First of all because one usually writes a letter before suing a man; secondly because if he complies with our demand, it will be cheaper all round. Now, if we're going to make a demand in our letter, I think it much better that that demand should be a demand with which he is bound to comply.'

'I suppose you know what you're talking about,' said the major, 'though I don't know why I suppose that. Sorry to be so blunt, but my and my family's experiences with lawyers have been disastrous. How much is all this going to cost me?'

'Well,' said Jane, 'if Mr Trotter has any money I don't think it will cost you anything.'

'What did you say?'

'Well, he'll have to pay the costs if he loses the action.'

'Suppose there isn't any action – suppose he hands over the machine at once?'

'Strictly speaking, you could sue him in order to get the costs of this interview and the letter I'm going to write, but you might not think it worth it.'

'And how much will it cost me if I don't? Do you charge by the minute? If so, I'd better stop talking or you'll be charging for what *I* say.'

'It'll only be a couple of guineas, Major Buttonstep, unless you consider that extortionate.'

'No,' the major admitted, 'that's not too bad. Well, suppose you write the letter and he doesn't hand the thing over. What happens next?'

'Well, if you agree, I shall then issue a summons on your behalf in the Copplestone County Court.'

'How long will all this take?'

'I'll get the letter off today. I shall call for the machine myself in three days' time.'

'It'd be too heavy for you.'

'Oh, of course. I don't know if …'

'Digby or John can go with you.'

'Oh, thank you, that would be very kind. Then, if he doesn't hand it over, the summons will be issued within two or three days and it should come up for hearing about six weeks later.'

'Six weeks!' said the major. 'You don't mean months or years, do you?'

'No – weeks.'

'Well, they've certainly speeded things up a bit since I had anything to do with the law. All right, Miss Coombe, please do as you suggest. I'm sorry I've been a bit impatient, but I've had a lot to put up with.'

Mr Trotter made no reply to Jane's letter, and in consequence she and John called at Mr Trotter's house at the time and day mentioned in the letter. They rang and knocked but there was no answer. They came away and within a week Mr Trotter had been served with a summons claiming the return of the machine and damages for its detention.

The summons told Mr Trotter to put in a defence to the claim if he had one. Mr Trotter did nothing. So Jane then obtained an order from the Court that he should put in a defence within seven days.

On the sixth day she received a letter from Mr Dealtry.

We have been consulted by our client, Mr Trotter, as to the summons issued against him in this matter. We have to inform you that we shall in due course be putting in a defence and counterclaim, and shall be obliged if you will extend our time for doing so for seven days as we have only recently been instructed.

Jane was rather taken aback by the counterclaim but she assumed it would be in respect of the major's attempt to break into Mr Trotter's house. That no doubt amounted to a technical trespass but Jane was quite satisfied that any damages awarded would be purely nominal. She talked to Prunella about it.

'You'd better come and do this, Pru, when it comes to trial.'

'Suppose I make a mess of it?'

'You mustn't. Anyway, it seems quite straightforward. The man's a lunatic obviously. We'd better ask father about the damages.'

Later that day they consulted Mr Justice Coombe.

'Well, it was a trespass to land,' he said, 'but if what your client says is right, it did no actual damage and, if the defendant has been hanging on to the mower without any justification, I can't see any judge awarding more than a few shillings. But it's a very odd case from what you tell me. I should wait till you see the defence and counterclaim itself. I'm not saying that your client is keeping anything back, but the story as a whole doesn't make sense unless, of course, the other chap is certifiable. Nearly always when I've had a case which didn't make sense there was something else behind it. When I was at the Bar I could usually force my client to tell me. On the Bench I have to wait till it turns up – but in most cases it does. No, there's something very odd about this. We haven't had the whole truth yet.'

'What sort of thing lies behind it, father?'

'Well, I've no idea and this is merely a guess. You tell me that Major Buttonstep and Mr Trotter were strangers to each other until this happened. Well, it's conceivable that they weren't and that there's a long-standing enmity between the two. That's doubtful but possible. Then, again, Buttonstep's almost pathological about lawyers, and Trotter seems a very odd individual indeed. It's possible that, though they themselves haven't met before, their families have clashed in litigation in the past. They may both know this, or possibly only one of them does. But there's something of the sort in this case. Otherwise things don't happen like this. They can happen between neighbours who hate each other, or are always quarrelling. They can happen with lunatics. But, from what I gather, neither of them is mad – well, no madder than any of us. We've all got kinks of some kind. Yes, perhaps Buttonstep's hatred of lawyers is a bit worse than any of my fads. But he didn't start this. We know that. If we only had his word for it, it might be different. But your two young men have both been concerned. And they're certainly sane. Are they, by the way, *your* two young men?'

'We hope so,' said Jane. 'D'you like them?'

'I've liked as much as I've seen of them.'

'They're really terribly nice,' said Prunella, 'and they're so sweet about their father. They're really worried about him.'

'How d'you mean?'

'Well – well – if we actually – I mean …'

'You mean if you became officially engaged?'

'Yes,' said the girls together. 'Would you be pleased?'

'I've always been pleased when you've been pleased – or nearly always anyway. And I'm sure I should be this time. But to come back to your case, Buttonstep's behaviour in trying to break into the house is a little unusual though, bearing in mind his hatred of going to law, I can't think what else a man in his condition of mind could do. He shouldn't have, of course, but I can understand it. Trotter's behaviour, on the other hand, is quite extraordinary. The doctor says he's quite sane and, if that's correct, I simply do not believe that a man would behave as he has – unless there were something behind it all. Of course, another possibility is that the man is in fact a raving lunatic and that the doctor's wrong.'

'How will all this affect the case?'

'Well, I don't know that it will really.'

'I thought you said you found that usually the truth emerged in such cases?'

'That is so. You may find, as the case goes on, either that Trotter is mad or that there's a feud between him and Buttonstep, or has been in the past between their families. But it won't affect your preparation of the case. Only I should try to find out tactfully from Buttonstep whether he has known Trotter in the past – or whether his family has known the Trotters. Of course, Trotter may not be the name in question and it may not mean anything to Buttonstep. You might find, for instance, that one of Trotter's maternal ancestors was engaged in a life and death struggle with one of the Buttonsteps. If that's so, it won't affect the result of the case. Except, I suppose, that the judge might award aggravated damages for the detention. He could do that anyway in view of the way Trotter's played about with him. But, if there were obvious malice as a result of some previous clash between the families, the judge could certainly add on a bit for that.'

'Well, suppose the major was guilty of malice when he tried to break into the house, he could add something for that, couldn't he?' asked Jane.

'How d'you mean?'

'Well, suppose Mr Trotter's just an eccentric and the major knows he is in fact a descendant of an enemy of the family – and tried to break in for that reason?'

'That seems a bit far-fetched. He couldn't have known what would happen when he lent the mowing machine, could he? Oh – well – I suppose theoretically he could have known that there was a taint in the Trotter family and that it was a habit of theirs to borrow things and make excuses for not returning them. But he didn't seek out Trotter. Trotter asked one of the boys for the loan. It would be a very odd coincidence if Trotter played into Buttonstep's hands like that. Anyway, Buttonstep is a perfectly ordinary chap except in his dislike of lawyers. And after all a lot of people dislike us. He's just a bit worse because his family have been confirmed litigants. No, I can't think that, whatever emerges, Buttonstep's going to have to pay more than forty shillings for his trespass.'

'He won't like paying that,' said Jane.

'Well, the judge may only put it at a shilling, but he'd be wise to pay the normal forty into Court. Then, unless the judge goes mad and awards more than forty, you're pretty well bound to get all the costs of the counterclaim. You'd better wait till you see it. Of course he might allege that your client damaged some old brickwork. But don't lose any sleep over it. When it comes to it, he may not put in any counterclaim at all. It's a trumpery matter anyway – his solicitor may dissuade him.'

'It isn't quite as trumpery as you say, daddy,' said Jane. 'Digby and John are terribly anxious not to have an official engagement without first making their father happy about it. If everything goes right with the action, he might think better of it.'

'Well, it's no good worrying. You'll have to wait till you see the counterclaim.'

And they had to. But, when it came, it made no complaint whatever about the major's attempted entry. It alleged something far more disturbing – slander.

'On the 14th June,' it said, 'the plaintiff falsely and maliciously spoke and published of and concerning the defendant to one Police Constable Glossop, the constable at Buttonstep, the words following, that is to say: "You" (meaning and being understood to mean the defendant) "are a thief or mad".' As if deliberately to goad the major the counterclaim went on to state the obvious by adding: 'By the said words the plaintiff meant and was understood to mean that either the defendant had stolen the plaintiff's mowing machine or that the defendant was of unsound mind.'

'Oh, dear,' said Prunella to Jane, when they read the fateful document, 'I can't conduct a slander action. I wouldn't know where to begin. I didn't know you could have one in a County Court.'

'You couldn't start one there, but you can put one in a counterclaim. Of course, we could apply to transfer the counterclaim or the whole action to the High Court, but I can't see the expense and delay involved appealing much to Major Buttonstep.'

'What are we to do?' said Prunella. 'He'll blow up when he hears of this. D'you think he said it?'

'I expect so,' said Jane, 'but I'd better ask him. Let's talk to father first, though.'

They spoke to the judge as soon as they could and told him what had happened.

'I see,' he said when he had read the document. 'Before he knows where he is Major Buttonstep will be well and truly involved in litigation.'

'Is there any defence to the claim, if he said it?'

'Oh, certainly,' said the judge, 'but whether it succeeds or not, will depend on what I was saying before. If Buttonstep had never heard of Trotter or his family before and was only angry with him because he wouldn't hand back the mower, you can rely on privilege as a defence – and I think you'd succeed. After all, if a man does behave like Trotter for no explained reason he is either mad or bad or possibly both, and a policeman is just the right person to inform. So, provided it wasn't said in malice, the claim should fail. But first of all you'd better find out if he said it.'

Jane decided to go to see the major rather than write to him. She could imagine the effect on him of receiving a letter which showed that his apparently simple little claim had grown into a slander action. So she arranged an appointment with him at his house, and as soon as they had exchanged greetings, she got to the point.

'We've had the counterclaim in, Major Buttonstep,' she began.

'How much do they want for my climbing up the wall? £1,000, eh?'

'They're not complaining of that.'

'Then what do they claim?'

'They say,' said Jane, 'that you said to PC Glossop that Mr Trotter had either stolen the machine or that he was mad.'

'So I did and so he is. What about it?'

'Well, they call it slander and ask for damages.'

'And what d'you call it?'

'Well,' said Jane, 'if we could prove he was mad or that he had sold the machine or something like that, we could prove it was true. But, if we can't prove either of these things, we'll have to rely on privilege.'

'Look,' said the major, 'here's a man borrows my mower, won't give it back, behaves like a lunatic whenever we ask for it, and you tell me that he can sue me because I say so? I've never heard of such nonsense.'

'Well, we can't stop him counterclaiming but, as I said, we can rely on the defence of privilege.'

'Why can't you lawyers talk English? What does that mean?'

'If you say something without malice to someone to whom you have a right or duty to say it, they can't sue you for it.'

'Well he has sued me or counterclaimed or whatever you call it.'

'I mean his claim won't succeed.'

'And how many extra hundred pounds is that going to cost me, may I ask?'

'Well, if he loses, it won't cost you anything – if he can pay the costs.'

'And suppose I lose?'

'I'm afraid that would be rather expensive,' said Jane.

'As I thought,' said the major. 'I'd have done much better to let him keep the beastly machine. I knew I was right. Now I'm up to my eyes in the law.'

'I think he's treated you abominably,' said Jane, 'and I really don't see why you should put up with it.'

'I dare say you don't,' said the major. 'Indeed, as a lawyer you wouldn't. If people put up with things there'd be no work for you. If I give up the claim to the mowing machine will he give up his claim for the slander, d'you think?'

'I should think he would, if he's sensible,' said Jane. 'But are you really going to make him a present of the machine?'

'What else can I do, my dear girl? Now, I'm not blaming you in any way. You've got your job to do and your living to earn. But we had a slander action in our family once. If you'll come with me, I'll show you some of the papers. It lasted three weeks in one Court and a week in another. It took two years or more altogether and both sides had forgotten what the slander was before we'd finished. We were both so busy paying our own lawyers we couldn't think of anything else.'

'Did your family win it?'

'Nobody won it, except the lawyers. It was settled in the end. After the week in the second Court the claim was withdrawn and each side paid its own costs. About £5,000 apiece, I suppose. Might have been more. That's what you call litigation. Somebody says something. Someone else goes to a lawyer and, in the end, the one that's said it has to pay £5,000 and so does the one he said it about. I wonder any of our family dared to open their mouths after that little affair. I'm not going to be saddled with £5,000, I tell you. He can have the blasted mowing machine and I'll never lend anything else to anyone so long as I live.'

'Well, then, major,' said Jane, 'your definite instructions are to agree to withdraw your claim if they'll withdraw theirs?'

'Definite,' said the major. 'I can feel the suction from the legal machine already. But I'm not going to be drawn in this time, even if it means giving in to that madman.' He paused. 'Does saying that to you cost me another £1,000?'

'Oh, no. What you say to me is absolutely privileged.'

'That's the word you used before. I thought you said I'd got to have a right or duty to say things before they're privileged.'

'This is a rather different privilege,' began Jane.

'Don't tell me,' said the major, 'otherwise I might understand too much of the law and wouldn't need your help. A different privilege!' he went on. 'Why do the public stand for it? Well, I won't anyway. The law is even worse than Mr Trotter. There's a limit to what he does – he just pinches a mowing machine. But the law would pinch everything I've got, if it had the chance. Are there many other kinds of privilege, by the way?'

'I'm afraid there are,' said Jane.

'Don't apologise,' said the major. 'You didn't invent them. Seen much of John lately?'

'Well, we did go to a theatre together last Thursday.'

'He's a nice boy. So's Digby. They're both decent boys. Why the devil they have to ... oh – never mind. Well, you'll settle the action for me, then?'

'Of course. I'll write at once.'

That evening the major told Digby and John that the proceedings were over. He explained why.

'I must say,' said Digby, 'I don't like the idea of his getting away with it. I'm hanged if I'd let him.'

Mr Justice Coombe's view that litigation was in the Buttonstep blood appeared to be right.

'I dare say you wouldn't,' said the major, 'but you haven't had my experience. But, dammit, you have seen what I showed you. Would you allow yourself to be sucked in after seeing all those? I don't care what my rights are, I'm not going to get involved. It was stupid of me to start in the first place. I might have realised what would happen. Anyway, it's over now, thank goodness. We'd better try to find a second-hand machine. I shan't be able

to afford a new one after paying your girlfriend's – I beg
your pardon – my solicitor's costs.'

Jane duly telephoned Mr Trotter's solicitor suggesting a
settlement of the proceedings.

'Put it in writing, please,' said Mr Dealtry, 'so that I can
show it to my client.'

So Jane wrote a letter, headed 'without prejudice':

Our client is very loath to be involved in heavy
litigation and he has accordingly instructed us that, if
your client will withdraw his counterclaim, he will
withdraw the claim. We shall be glad to hear that
your client agrees to these terms before further costs
are incurred.

On receipt of the letter Mr Dealtry telephoned his client
and in consequence Mr Trotter came to see him the next
day.

'Well,' said Mr Trotter, 'that's fine. They've got the wind
up.'

'D'you want me to accept the suggestion?' asked Mr
Dealtry, a little anxiously. Although he was a man of
complete integrity, he did not like settlements. He would
try to keep his clients out of litigation but, once started, he
liked to see it brought to a finish in the Courts. He had
indeed tried to prevent Mr Trotter from defending the
action. He had warned him that he had no defence and
that it would be much cheaper to hand over the machine
and to pay the small costs incurred up to service of the
summons. But Mr Trotter had obstinately refused and,
when Mr Dealtry found that, although he might have no
defence to the action he had a possible slander action, his
attitude changed a little. First of all, he had assured
himself that the machine was still in his client's

possession, and then he had persuaded his client to allow himself to be examined by two doctors – a general physician and a psychiatrist. Both had been of the opinion that their patient was quite sane. In those circumstances it was at least possible that there would be an award of damages exceeding the costs of the claim for the return of the mowing machine. But, before advising his client, he had consulted counsel.

As far as Mr Dealtry was concerned there was only one practising barrister – Romilly Larpent. The Law List contained many other names, 2,000 of them practising, but from the time Mr Dealtry had first instructed Mr Larpent no one else would do. If he could not do a case, it would have to be adjourned until he could. Litigation without Mr Larpent was unthinkable. This was not because of any particular degree of excellence which Mr Larpent possessed; it was simply because Mr Dealtry thought he possessed it. There are indeed other solicitors, who insist upon instructing counsel of proved incompetence, but none of them equalled Mr Dealtry in his determination to have no one but Mr Larpent appearing for his clients.

Romilly Larpent was an amiable man of reasonable ability but long-winded to a degree which made some judges quail when they saw that he had a case before them. But his chief defect was an overwhelming courtesy. It is a difficult feat to be too courteous but Romilly Larpent brought it off easily. Judges, counsel and even sometimes witnesses squirmed before his respectful submissions, objections or questions as the case might be. He was in a perpetual state of being, if he might say so, very much obliged indeed.

He would profusely thank a witness who had given an awkward answer and his ingratiating and toothy smile on such occasions strongly suggested that he felt under a deep obligation to the person concerned. He would express himself as being exceedingly grateful to his learned opponent for pointing out the obvious. And finally he would be deeply indebted, if he might say so, to the learned judge for listening so patiently to his argument and entirely disregarding it.

When Mr Dealtry had first approached him to advise about *Buttonstep v Trotter*, he had been most grateful to him for setting out his instructions so clearly.

'It is such an advantage to counsel,' he had said, 'to know exactly what he is dealing with. If I may say so, you make the position very plain, indeed beyond a peradventure, beyond a peradventure.'

'What d'you advise, Mr Larpent?'

'Ah, that's a question, isn't it? Naturally you want to start on the right foot. Naturally. Very proper, if I may say so.'

'Have we any defence to the claim?'

'That's a question too, isn't it? Have we? Or haven't we?'

'That's the question, Mr Larpent. As usual, you've got to the heart of the matter at once.'

'Oh, that was nothing at all,' Mr Larpent had said modestly. 'How could I do otherwise with such instructions, if I may respectfully say so?'

'That's very nice of you.'

'Not at all. I really am most grateful.'

'And do you see any defence to the claim?'

'I find none in the instructions.'

'I could see none, Mr Larpent, but I wondered if you could find one.'

'It's unlikely, if I may say so,' Mr Larpent had replied, 'that I should be able to find what you couldn't. Indeed, if I might say so, it was not just unlikely but in the highest degree improbable – indeed, if it is not going too far, it is impossible.'

'That's most gratifying, but I didn't want to leave any stone unturned.'

'I'm quite sure you've left none, Mr Dealtry. Where nothing is, nothing can be found.'

'You're quite sure of that?'

'The facts, as your instructions so clearly demonstrate, are too plain. The mower belongs to the plaintiff, demands for its return have been made and not complied with. Why won't he give it up, Mr Dealtry?'

'He says he will in his own good time, and that he would have done so before if the plaintiff hadn't slandered him.'

'Two wrongs, if I may say so, do not make a right, Mr Dealtry.'

'Exactly what I said, Mr Larpent. He says he wants to set off the damages he gets for the slander against the value of the mowing machine.'

'Well, Mr Dealtry, I doubt if that's possible in any event. But, if the judge orders the return of the machine as, in my – I think I may say our – view he undoubtedly will, I don't see how he can set off anything against that.'

'Exactly. Just what I said, Mr Larpent.'

'Well, perhaps if you tell him that I agree – most profoundly, if I may say so – with your view, he will alter his own and hand the machine back. I fear that he will only have to pay the costs if he doesn't.'

'Well, I'll try again, Mr Larpent. Now, what about the slander? We're on firmer ground there, I hope?'

'Much firmer, Mr Dealtry.'

'What defence can there be? They can never prove our client tried to steal the machine, or that he's mad.'

'I suppose they might rely on privilege.'

'For words spoken in anger, Mr Larpent?'

'If he believed them to be true his anger would not matter.'

'But if he only said them in anger without having any particular belief about the matter?'

'Ah, that would be a different kettle of fish, Mr Dealtry. Indeed, yet once again, if I may say so, you have put your finger on the point. Everything depends on whether he really believed what he was saying to be true or whether he just said what he did because he was angry.'

'What about mere vulgar abuse, Mr Larpent?'

'Yes, that is a point to be considered, Mr Dealtry. One has to think it over. Undoubtedly. Mere vulgar abuse.'

'In other words, did he really mean it?'

'If I might very respectfully disagree there, Mr Dealtry, if you'll forgive me – isn't it rather a question of how the words were understood? If the policeman didn't think he meant it, and thought it was mere abuse, that would, if I may say so, be one thing. But if, although he didn't in fact mean what he said, the policeman really thought he did, mere vulgar abuse would surely be no defence? I say this, of course, subject to anything further you may say on the matter, Mr Dealtry, and without in any way trying to suggest that my view is more likely to be right than yours.'

'You are obviously right, Mr Larpent. How did the policeman understand the words? Assuming him, of course, to be a reasonable man.'

'Exactly, Mr Dealtry, and, if I may say so, most policemen, if not all, are likely to be reasonable men. Except, of course, when they run you in for obstruction. Just a joke, Mr Dealtry, just a joke.'

'Then you think we should win on the counterclaim, Mr Larpent?'

' "Should" is rather a strong word, Mr Dealtry. "Might" certainly, "could" certainly, "may" certainly – that's really the same as "might" for this purpose, isn't it? But "should" or "shall" are too strong. If the judge takes the view that the plaintiff had no belief in the truth of what he was saying, then we shall win. If *aliter, contra* – by which I mean …'

'I quite understand, Mr Larpent, and am most grateful to you for such a concise and definite opinion. My client will, I am sure, be most grateful.'

Mr Trotter had indeed appeared very grateful. 'But they're cautious devils, these barristers,' he said. 'He doesn't like to say we'll win in case we lose. Doesn't like to say we'll lose in case we win. What d'you think yourself, Mr Dealtry?'

'I do not think Mr Larpent could have put it better. I think as he does exactly.'

'Well, neither of you will ever be wrong if you go on like that,' Mr Trotter had said. 'But that suits me. I'm frightened of people who are too sure of themselves. If you'd both said I was bound to win I should have doubted it. If you'd both said I was bound to lose I'd have thought you were gloomy devils who always looked on the dark side. As it is, I know just where I am, don't I?'

'Quite,' Mr Dealtry had said, although he was not entirely sure where that was.

'In the middle of the deep blue sea smiling,' Mr Trotter had said, as if he could read Mr Dealtry's thoughts.

So the counterclaim was duly put in and Mr Dealtry (with the help of Mr Larpent) started to prepare for trial. And then he suddenly had Jane's offer of a settlement. To most people it would have seemed a good solution. Mr Trotter was bound to lose the claim for the mower and, in view of his obstinacy, he would have to pay the costs of it.

If he won his claim for slander, the damages in the circumstances would be unlikely to exceed the costs of the claim by much, if at all. If both claim and counterclaim were now abandoned all Mr Trotter would have to do would be to pay his own costs up to date, and he would be comforted by the thought that Major Buttonstep would have to pay his own costs. But Mr Dealtry, who had started to prepare for the trial of the case, did not like the idea at all. Nevertheless he knew that he would feel it his duty to point out to his client that it was in fact a good solution. First, however, he waited to see his client's immediate reaction.

'Yes,' said Mr Dealtry, 'it's very odd that they should offer to give up what seems to be a cast-iron claim – unless they're really worried about the slander.'

'Suppose we agreed, who keeps the mower?' asked Mr Trotter.

'Well, it belongs to Major Buttonstep.'

'We know that. But I've got it. Who keeps it?'

'Well – you ought to give it back to him.'

'Suppose I don't?'

'Well, he *could*, I imagine, sue you again.'

'What! After having abandoned the claim?'

'That's a nice point. I should have to speak to Mr Larpent about that. But there's no doubt that Major Buttonstep owns the mower.'

'But there's also no doubt that he hasn't got it. Why shouldn't he be giving it to me instead of paying damages for what he said?'

'That is a point of view, Mr Trotter,' said Mr Dealtry. 'I'll have to consider it.'

'I shouldn't bother,' said Mr Trotter.

'But I shall have to. Indeed I shall. You've raised a most important point. You don't want to be sued again.'

'I won't be sued again,' said Mr Trotter.

'How can you tell?'

'Because I'm not accepting his offer. We'll finish it off this time.'

'It's only right that I should warn you that, in that case, you're sure to have to give up the mower, whereas, if you accept his suggestion, you might – I only say might, mind you – be able to keep it.'

Mr Dealtry put the position very fairly to his client but hoped that his warning would in no way alter his client's point of view. His honesty was rewarded and his hopes fulfilled.

'He started the thing and now he's got to finish it. You all said I ought to hand the machine back to him. You begged me to. Told me that all sorts of things might happen if I didn't. Order of the judge to return. Prison if I didn't. Now look what's happened. He's offered to cry the whole thing off. That, Mr Dealtry, is the time to keep the whole thing on. We'll fight Major Buttonstep all the way. No quarter, no parley. He wanted a fight. He shall have it. I'd return a very curt answer to that letter, but you lawyers have to observe the courtesies, I suppose.'

'Yes, indeed.'

'Quite so. Then will you please tell the gallant gentleman in whatever legal language you may choose that my answer to him is … well, you know what.'

Accordingly, Mr Dealtry was delighted to reply to Jane's letter as follows:

We have consulted our client about your offer but he is not prepared to consider any compromise. Both claim and counterclaim must accordingly proceed to trial.

Jane wondered how Major Buttonstep would take the news, and was not quite sure how to break it to him. If he had just been an ordinary client, it would have been easy enough. But, as she wanted him as a father-in-law, it was a different matter. She decided to do it in person, rather than telephone or write a letter, but, as soon as the interview began, she wished she'd adopted either of the alternative courses.

'Well, young lady, you've come for your money, I suppose? I must say you lawyers don't take long to ask for your fees. Latest idea's to call for them, is it? Frightened I'd run away or something?'

'It isn't about the costs, Major Buttonstep. I'm afraid they won't settle the action. It's got to go on.'

'What nonsense are you talking? I'm bringing the case, aren't I? I can stop it if I want to.'

'Oh, yes, of course, but, if you simply do that without their agreeing to withdraw their counterclaim, you'll not only have to pay their costs but they will go on with their claim just the same. And you could only stop that, I imagine, by paying their damages.'

'This is outrageous!' said the major. 'I'll pay them no damages. Damages for what, I ask you? It's that madman who owes me damages.'

'Then the counterclaim will continue, even if you drop the claim.'

'There's a lawyer behind this. You mark my words. What have I always said? The legal machine will suck you in if it gets the chance. And, by Jove, I can feel its tentacles round me now. Get me out of it young lady, please. I know what'll happen if you don't. The same as to my great-great-grandfather. We'll be taken through all the Courts and ruined again. Get me out of it, I say!'

'Well, I'll have another try, Major Buttonstep,' said Jane, 'but I can't make them settle. You can give in altogether if you want to, but it seems very hard on you to do that when you're in the right and it would be quite expensive.'

'How much?' asked the major.

'I'll find out,' said Jane.

'You do that, please. I'm not going to get sucked in.' In consequence of the major's instructions, Jane telephoned Mr Dealtry and, 'without prejudice,' asked him what his client would want to settle the whole proceedings. Mr Dealtry was really surprised and again rather sad that what looked like a fight seemed likely to collapse. However, at least he could insist on all his costs being paid, and he would have the satisfaction of being able to say that, in a case which he felt sure would be lost as far as the claim was concerned, he had brought the other side to his knees. He reported the good news to Mr Trotter.

'How much do I want to settle,' mused Mr Trotter. 'Let me see. I'll want the mower, my costs and – what shall we say? £1,500 damages?'

'But really, Mr Trotter,' said Mr Dealtry, 'even if you won the action, you'd never get that.'

'How can you tell?'

'No judge would ever give it.'

'Why not? Slandering me to the local policeman's a very serious matter. Anyway, it's obvious they don't want it brought to Court and they'll pay to prevent it. Sting them till they howl for mercy. You can knock off a couple of hundred, if you like.'

A few days later Jane reported to the major what it would cost him to settle the proceedings.

'I might get them to reduce the damages a bit,' she said, 'but not very much, I'm afraid.'

The major did not reply for a moment or two. He was almost stunned by the information. A man borrows his mower, refuses to hand it back, and the suggested settlement of his righteous claim was that he should give up his mower and pay at the least something over £1,000.

'If you like,' said Jane, 'I'll ask my father what he thinks.'

To her surprise the major, after a few moments' thought, said that it would be very kind of her to do so. It was a considerable decision for him to have to make, but much as he disliked the idea of being beholden to a judge for anything, he disliked even more the possibility of having to pay anything to Mr Trotter.

So, as soon as she could, Jane went back to her father and told him what had happened.

'I told you there was something behind this,' was his first reply. 'But what it is I really have no idea. Let me think. The plaintiff decides to abandon his claim if the claim for slander is also abandoned. The defendant then asks absurd damages for the slander. Why did the major take fright so easily? Even if the counterclaim for slander succeeded, the damages wouldn't be very high. Then why does the defendant, by asking ridiculous damages, pretty well compel the plaintiff to go on with the case – when he must have been advised that he has no answer to the claim and might lose his counterclaim? I suppose the answer to the first question could be that it was the sudden fear of getting caught up in litigation which made him prefer to give up his claim. Knowing what you've said about him, I think that's a reasonable possibility. But I shouldn't bank on it, because I simply can't find any explanation for the defendant's behaviour – unless he's mad. The most he could possibly get for the slander – the very most, would be a hundred or two and in fact he might lose the counterclaim altogether, indeed he very likely will. Why then does he reject this very good offer of a settlement and counter-offer ridiculous terms? It's beyond me at the moment, but you must watch for something odd to turn up somewhere. I repeat, I do not for one moment believe that we know the whole truth of this matter. There is something odder than ever about it. As to what you should do – well that at the moment is pretty simple. Tell your client that he's not bound to fight, if he doesn't want to do so, but that he'd be very foolish if he complied with the defendant's suggestion or anything like it – provided, of course, that he's telling you the whole truth about the matter.'

'I hardly like to suggest he isn't or may not be,' said Jane.

'I see that,' said her father, 'but, if I were you, I should say something of the kind as tactfully as possible. After all, when the bombshell falls, as I feel reasonably sure that it will some time, you, as a solicitor, will be in a position to say that you did warn your client of the necessity of telling you everything.'

So Jane saw the major again.

'I suppose,' she began, 'there isn't anything to do with the case which I don't know?'

'How can I tell? You're the lawyer. I don't know what you do have to know.'

'No – I mean about the facts. Has anything happened between you and Mr Trotter which you might have forgotten to tell me?'

'Well, if I've forgotten it, I shouldn't remember it, should I?'

'Perhaps you remember it now?'

'I didn't say there was anything.'

'Or anything between your families?' Jane went on.

'Between our families? What on earth d'you mean? I've never known the fellow. As far as I'm concerned he hasn't got any family.'

'Could one of his ancestors have lived in Buttonstep, by any chance?'

'How on earth should I know? All I know about him is that he says his name's Trotter – and he's got my mower.'

'He might have a grudge against you of some kind.'

'Why should he? I've got one against him.'

'Something you've forgotten might have taken place between you in the past.'

'I tell you I don't know the chap! Until he put his head out of the window I'd never seen him before in my life.'

'But he could, for example, be the descendant of a family who had had a quarrel with one of your family, and he might have come to Buttonstep to pay off an old score.'

'I see what you mean. You think the whole thing was engineered from the start out of spite?'

'Something of the kind.'

'Well, that does make sense. I'll look up some of the old papers. But, come to think of it, that may not help. Not without this fellow's family tree. Anyway, let's go and look.'

He took Jane to his study and opened the cupboard where the remains of ancient hatreds were stored. He looked through the papers for about ten minutes.

'I can't even find one that begins with a T.'

'I'm afraid it's only an off-chance. And, of course, you're quite right in saying that it's impossible without Mr Trotter's family tree to tell whether he's a descendant of any of these people. I can ask his solicitors, of course, but I don't suppose they'll tell me. Still I can try, unless you'd rather I didn't.'

But the major had found something that interested him, and was not listening.

'Just look at this bill of costs,' he said. 'It's a work of art, I must say.'

It was dated 1859 and must indeed have taken the clerk who had written it out in flawless script many hours to produce. 'A labour of love, no doubt,' said the major, forgetting that the man who drew up the bill was probably grossly underpaid and received none of the profits.

'Nothing's forgotten, you see. "To attending you at your house (4³/₄ miles each way) for the purpose of discussing with you in detail a variation of your daughter's settlement upon which you had asked us to advise you but your butler said on your behalf that it was not convenient to see you. £5 5s 0d." Note the "on your behalf." They weren't taking any chances that the butler did it off his own bat. But I'm sorry – we came here to look for Trotter. What was it you said?'

Jane repeated her suggestion.

'Well, there's no harm in asking,' said the major. 'We can make up our minds about what to do when you've had an answer.'

So the next day Jane wrote to Mr Dealtry:

Your client's behaviour in this matter has been so extraordinary that it occurs to us and our client that there may have been some quarrel in the past between our client's family and your client's. Is your client prepared to instruct you to let us know whether this is the case or not or alternatively to let us know the names of his ancestors on both sides of his family as far as he is able to do so?

Mr Dealtry at once interviewed his client on the matter.

'Cheek,' said Mr Trotter, 'isn't it?'

'It is certainly the oddest request I've ever seen in my life. I've asked the other side a lot of questions in my time, but never for their family tree.'

'Can't we make something of it?' suggested Mr Trotter. 'Isn't the suggestion that I'm actuated by spite?'

'You've got a point there, Mr Trotter.'

'Could we sue them in respect of this letter? Can we say it's libellous?'

'Well,' said Mr Dealtry, 'I'd have to see Mr Larpent about that. The letter is written by solicitors and they certainly haven't any spite against you.'

'But if their client has, does that make any difference?'

'Let me see,' said Mr Dealtry, and went to his shelves and fetched a law book. 'Oh, dear,' he said, after a few minutes, 'it raises a very difficult point. There's *Smith and Streatfield* – but that wouldn't mean anything to you, of course. I'm sorry.'

'How much does it mean to you?' asked Mr Trotter.

Although Major Buttonstep would have had difficulty in approving anything that Mr Trotter did, he might have had a little pleasure at seeing Mr Dealtry's tail being twisted about the law.

'It's not too easy,' said Mr Dealtry. 'I think I'll have to leave it to Mr Larpent.'

'Well, don't bother for the moment,' said Mr Trotter. 'We can keep it up our sleeves for use later on if necessary.'

'What shall I reply about your family tree?'

'You first tell them,' said Mr Trotter, 'that I am not prepared to discuss with them where I was born, when I was born, of whom I was born or why I was born, nor am I prepared to disclose where I buy my shirts or my shoes, where I get my hair cut, what television programmes I most enjoy, what my politics are or which Church I attend. In other words, tell them to go to Hell.'

'Certainly,' said Mr Dealtry. 'But just for my own private information, in case anything should ever arise on it, I would like to know whether there ever has been any sort of a quarrel between your respective families?'

Mr Trotter hesitated a moment.

'Mr Dealtry,' he said, 'I prefer to ride you in blinkers.'

'Really, sir!' said Mr Dealtry, 'that is not a very courteous way in which to address your attorney.'

'I'm sorry,' said Mr Trotter. 'No offence intended. But, if it's got nothing to do with the case, why should I delve into my family history? You mustn't infer from my attitude that there is anything to delve into, but, if my great-great-aunt on my father's side did once resist the advances of Major Buttonstep's great-great-uncle on his mother's side by poking a knitting needle in his eye, why should I add to their souls' torment by talking of the matter today? Just think of them both in purgatory being cleansed of this particular sin. For unquestionably it was a sin on both sides. No doubt Buttonstep's great-great-uncle should not have made the advance. It was inexcusable. My great-great-aunt had given him no encouragement. Perhaps dropping a handkerchief, a slight flutter of the eyelids – nothing more. Certainly no just cause for him to sound the charge. But, on the other hand, he was a small man and she was a well-built and, for those days, athletic young woman. She could have held his great-great-uncle down with one hand and rung the bell for assistance with the other. Instead, she said: "If you take one more step forward, sir, I will poke my needle in your eye." He did, and she did. I admit it was very wrong of her. Well, there they are in purgatory having the whole thing explained to them. My great-great-aunt is having explained to her the biological reasons why Buttonstep's great-great-uncle sounded the charge, and he is having explained to him why he should have resisted the sudden urge. It is all being done very nicely and quietly by experts. They are really getting somewhere. And suddenly they see the whole thing raked up on earth again. Because personally I'm sure that's what purgatory is in part – to hear how people talk about you six months after you've gone. The first few days are all right. You were good and noble and your loss is deeply lamented by your nearest and dearest and your hosts of friends. But after six months or so some people start to say what they really thought of you, occasionally adding – after some particularly biting piece of criticism – "but, of course, *de mortuis* and all that." After two or three years, they don't even bother to add that, while after ten years or so your nearest and dearest may even write your biography – described by the publishers as "full and frank" – calling public attention to some of your worst faults and some of the episodes in your life which you had hoped would be allowed to be forgotten. So there they are in purgatory, suffering very properly no doubt but hoping that that particular episode of the knitting needle had been forgotten. And suddenly they hear us or see us talking about it, laughing about it perhaps, and certainly embellishing it. By the time we've finished with it, Buttonstep's great-great-uncle, who never actually touched my great-great-aunt, has leaped upon her with unexampled ferocity and lust, while later she is seen sitting by the side of the unconscious great-great-uncle (he must have banged his head against the table as he leaped) calmly gouging out one of his eyes with one hand while she sips a cup of chocolate with the other. No, Mr Dealtry, I think we should leave our ancestors to purge their sins without our assistance.'

'I take it,' said Mr Dealtry, 'that there is no truth in that particular episode?'

'How do I know?' replied Mr Trotter. 'I may have had a great-great-aunt who knew Buttonstep's great-great-uncle. Admittedly, it would be an odd coincidence if something that I have invented out of my imagination should turn out to have been true, but I certainly cannot say that it is not true.'

'I understand,' said Mr Dealtry. 'And, as far as you know, there have been no such episodes between members of your family and members of the Buttonsteps'?'

'As I said before,' said Mr Trotter, 'I am not going to discuss that matter. I am prepared to go as far as saying that I do not believe the episode I have related between my great-great-aunt and Buttonstep's great-great-uncle ever took place, but, beyond that, I am not prepared to discuss the matter with anyone – unless, of course, it is necessary to do so for the purpose of these proceedings. But I repeat, you must not assume from my saying that that there is anything on this particular subject to discuss.'

'Very well,' said Mr Dealtry, 'I will write to the plaintiff's solicitors accordingly.'

Dear Sirs, *he wrote*,

You describe our client's behaviour as extraordinary. Whilst we resent this suggestion, which is quite unjustified, if there had been extraordinary behaviour on the part of our client, it has been more than matched by the letter which your client has instructed you to write. We can only reply that we are not aware of any quarrel between our client's and your client's families but we should make it plain that we have no intention whatever of going into this question with our client. This is not because we believe that, if we did so, we should ascertain that there have been any such quarrels but simply because we consider your client's request is irrelevant as well as being insolent. We further give you notice that our client reserves his rights against your client for any defamatory meaning there may be in your letter under reply. Finally, we should add that your client is perfectly entitled to consult a genealogical expert to enquire into our client's family if he wishes to do so but our client is not prepared to give any assistance in the matter.

Jane sent a copy of the letter to the major, who went to his wife for comfort. He was almost in tears.

'Look at this,' he said. 'They "reserve their rights." D'you know what it means? I do. It means that there may be more actions, more lawyers. What shall I do, what shall I do?'

'Poor darling,' said Mrs Buttonstep, 'I don't suppose it's as bad as you think. Lawyers bark a lot, but they don't always bite.'

'That's rather good,' said the major, brightening up a bit. 'I wish I'd thought of that.'

'You did, darling,' said his wife, 'a few weeks ago. I remembered it.'

'Well, I suppose there's nothing for it, old girl. We shall have to fight. I wouldn't pay out £1,000 to the fellow if I could afford it, and I can't afford it anyway. I'll have a final word with Digby and John, and see what they say.'

So that evening the Buttonsteps had a family conference and they all agreed that, unpleasant as the alternatives were, they must go ahead with the action.

'If it's any help, father,' said Digby, 'I've done pretty well recently and …'

'Nonsense,' said the major, 'I wouldn't hear of it. Anyway, John's friend says it won't cost me anything if we win.'

That night Prunella and Jane discussed the case again with their father.

'I think it would be a good idea,' he said, 'if you tried to get the defendant to admit the claim. Then he'll have to go into the witness box first. In a case like this, where something odd may turn up at any moment, it's important that you should be able to cross-examine the defendant before your client is cross-examined.'

'But from the way they've conducted the correspondence,' said Prunella, 'they won't admit anything.'

'Well, you can always interrogate them,' said the judge.

'One doesn't often have interrogatories in the County Court,' said Jane.

'I dare say you don't,' said the judge, 'and I don't suppose they're often any use. But here they might be. It could undoubtedly save costs if the demand for the return of the machine and the failure to comply with the demand were admitted. That's a good ground for applying for leave to interrogate. You try it.'

So Jane wrote a letter to Mr Dealtry, asking him if he would admit the claim on behalf of his client and, on receiving the expected refusal, she issued an application in the Copplestone County Court for leave to administer interrogatories to the defendant.

The application was heard in his private room by Mr Registrar Creamer. Mr Creamer had been a County Court registrar for many years and had nearly reached the retiring age. He had mellowed somewhat but in his younger days he had been what he himself would have described as a live wire. He was also very proud of his position as a County Court registrar and took pains to explain to anyone whom he met what his position really was.

There are, in fact, a good many registrars in this country, but most people think of a registrar in connection with the registration of births, deaths and marriages. Mr Creamer deeply resented any suggestion that that was his job, necessary to the community though it is. There are also medical registrars, registrars of companies, the Registrar of Friendly Societies and quite a number of legal registrars in addition to County Court registrars. A County Court registrar has judicial and administrative duties. He is responsible for the entire administration of the Court, but his judicial work takes up the greater part of his time. He tries small cases, and most applications in the course of a case, before it comes on for hearing by the judge, are made to the registrar.

So it came about that Jane's application came before Mr Registrar Creamer. She decided that she would conduct the application herself and so Mr Trotter was represented by Mr Dealtry. Although their presence was not necessary, both Major Buttonstep and Mr Trotter attended the hearing. As soon as everyone had been provided with a chair the registrar opened the proceedings. In his younger days he had been inclined to open and indeed sometimes to close them almost before the parties had entered the room. Although he was a lawyer, he considered himself a practical man, and he rather prided himself on his ability to avoid technical legal rules and to get down to the root of a matter. The younger you are, the quicker you think you can do this. Mr Registrar Creamer had slowed up considerably by the time Jane's application came before him.

'Well, what's all this about?' he began.

That had always been his opening, but, when he first started, he said it as the parties came through the door, decided what it was about just before they reached his desk and sometimes gave his decision before they had time to sit down.

'It's an application for leave to administer interrogatories,' said Jane.

'Yes, I see that,' said the registrar, 'but what is the whole thing about? What's this about a mower? And slander, too! This is getting out of hand. Tell me in a nutshell what it's all about.'

'In a nutshell,' said Jane, 'the defendant borrowed the plaintiff's mower, and won't give it back.'

'Why not?' asked the registrar.

'I suggest you ask Mr Dealtry that,' said Jane.

'Well, why not, Mr Dealtry?' asked the registrar.

Mr Dealtry coughed.

'Why not?' repeated the registrar.

'Well,' began Mr Dealtry, 'well – well, sir, wouldn't it be better if my learned friend opened her application?'

'No, Mr Dealtry, it would not. Interrogatories should only be administered if they are necessary and ...'

'Precisely,' said Mr Dealtry, 'and I'm going to submit to you, sir, that in this case ...'

'If you will let me finish, Mr Dealtry, please,' broke in the registrar. 'If you've got no defence to a claim, it's ridiculous to have it held up by writing down a lot of questions and putting in a lot of answers. If the truth of the matter is that you've got no defence, the sooner you say so the better. I'm not going to have a lot of time wasted by interrogatories. I grant you, they're usually a waste of time. But in this case it looks as though it was worth coming here, if you refused to admit the claim. Did you ask for an admission first, Miss Coombe?'

'Oh, certainly,' said Jane, 'and it was refused.'

'Well, Mr Dealtry,' said the registrar, 'is it the plaintiff's mower?'

'Well, yes, it is.'

'Has your client got it?'

'Yes.'

'Has he been asked to hand it over?'

'Well – he wasn't actually very well when he was …'

'Has he been asked to hand it over?' persisted the registrar.

'Well, yes, he has.'

'Then why doesn't he?'

There was a pause. The registrar repeated the question.

Major Buttonstep began to have a high regard for Mr Registrar Creamer. It was the first time he had seen so much good sense associated with the law. Of course, people who find a judge on their side usually think what a good judge he is.

'He would have, if the plaintiff hadn't slandered him, sir.'

'So slander's an answer to detinue, is it? What's your authority for that, Mr Dealtry?'

'I didn't say there was an authority for that proposition. I said that was why the plaintiff wouldn't hand over the mower.'

'Well, will he hand it over now?'

Mr Dealtry whispered to Mr Trotter and, having had a whispered reply, said that his client would not hand it over.

'Not even if the plaintiff apologises for the slander or whatever it was? This is a storm in a teacup, Mr Dealtry. Ought never to have got into solicitors' hands, let alone come to Court. But, now it's here, let's get it over and done with. The defendant will hand over the mower, the plaintiff will apologise. No order as to costs. How's that?'

'Remind him of Magna Carta,' whispered Mr Trotter to Mr Dealtry.

'I'm sorry. I heard that,' said the registrar. 'I'm proposing to give you a good deal more than Magna Carta. You want a full-scale action with counsel and solicitors on both sides and all the rest of it, do you? That's what Magna Carta gives you. And it says there's to be no delay. Well, you'll find no delay in this Court. But it's expensive. Magna Carta says nothing about not being expensive. To no one will we sell – well, there are no bribes in this country – to no one will we deny – to no one will we delay justice. Nothing about not charging, is there? Selling's quite another matter. Now I offer you something much better than that. Hand over the mower and shake hands. Be your age, gentlemen. You're not at school any longer. I feel like a mother with her children: "He's got my toy, mummy": "Give it back, darling": "Won't": "You should say shan't, darling, if that's what you mean": "Won't": "Well, you shouldn't say either really. Give it him back now." '

'Won't,' said Mr Trotter aloud.

'You mustn't talk to the learned registrar like that,' said Mr Dealtry sternly.

'Well, he shouldn't talk to me like that,' said Mr Trotter. 'This is supposed to be a Court of Law, not a kindergarten.'

'It feels more like a kindergarten,' said the registrar, 'when I have silly disputes like this to deal with.'

'I think I shall report you to whoever one does report people in your position to,' said Mr Trotter.

'It's the Lord Chancellor,' said the registrar. 'You are very welcome. Now, let's get on, please. I'm not prepared to waste very much more time on this. Yes, Mr Dealtry, I said "waste" – and your client can tell that to the Lord Chancellor too. Now what's it going to be? If you're not going to settle the action like sensible adults I shall have to make some kind of an order.'

Mr Dealtry consulted Mr Trotter. Jane spoke to the major.

'I'm afraid settlement is out of the question,' said Mr Dealtry.

'Oh, very well,' said the registrar. 'Now do you formally admit that there has been demand and refusal, and that the plaintiff was at all material times entitled to immediate possession of this machine?'

'He was only entitled to possession after demand, with respect, sir,' ventured Mr Dealtry.

'But there was a demand, was there not?'

'Oh, yes, sir.'

'Then why is the claim not admitted?'

'There was no actual refusal, sir. I admit a failure to deliver up after a demand, but no refusal.'

'You mean your client didn't say "I won't," as he did here, but he just didn't hand it over after being asked – although he could have done so.'

'Ah, that's the point, sir,' said Mr Dealtry. 'It's a very heavy machine. I do not admit that, in the circumstances, he could have delivered it up.'

'We offered to come in and take it away,' said Jane, 'but the defendant wouldn't even agree to this.'

'Is that correct, Mr Dealtry?'

'Yes sir.'

'What excuse was there for that?'

'The defendant was under no legal duty to allow the plaintiff to go through his premises.'

'But you agree he was liable to hand over the machine on the demand being made?'

'Yes, sir.'

'Then he should have got some able-bodied person to do it on his behalf.'

'He had no one on the premises capable of doing it. His failure to hand over did not, therefore, constitute refusal.'

'Very well,' said the registrar. 'How will this suit you, Miss Coombe? The defendant admitting that the plaintiff before action brought – demanded at the premises of the defendant – where the machine was at the time of such demand – the return of the said machine, and that the defendant failed to deliver up the same to the plaintiff, no order except costs in cause. Will that do?'

'Yes, thank you, sir,' said Jane.

'Any criticism of that, Mr Dealtry?'

'No, sir.'

'Very well then. I apologise to your client, Miss Coombe, for the ridiculous waste of time and for the somewhat technical language I have had to use, but the defendant's childish attitude in the matter leaves me no alternative. Good morning.'

The parties and their representatives left the registrar's room. The major was extremely pleased.

'It's a pity he's not trying the case,' he said. 'I suppose it would be impossible to arrange that?'

'It could only be done with Mr Trotter's consent and, in the circumstances, I can't see him consenting.'

'I must say he seemed a very sensible fellow. He sorted out Master Trotter pretty quickly. I hope the judge will do the same.'

'So do I,' said Jane.

Outside the Court Mr Trotter had a word with Mr Dealtry.

'Has he been got at, d'you think?' asked Mr Trotter. 'He was against us from the start.'

'Of course not,' said Mr Dealtry. 'Both Mr Larpent and I have warned you that there's no real defence to this claim. If you're wise you'll give it up and go ahead only on the slander.'

'Don't you believe it,' said Mr Trotter. 'Fight them all the way, please. My back is broad. A few criticisms from a registrar won't kill me.'

'The judge may be equally critical and his remarks will be made in public and may be reported.'

'Why should that worry me? What's a judge anyway? I know what I'm doing.'

'I suppose so,' said Mr Dealtry. 'You wouldn't like me to see if their offer of settlement is still open?'

'Good gracious, no,' said Mr Trotter. 'You go straight ahead. I'll have them on their knees before we've finished with them. You wait till we get those two sons of his in the box. They'll have to tell the truth, won't they?'

'Well, they'll be under oath. I expect they'll tell the truth. I can't guarantee it, of course.'

'It'll be perjury if they don't, won't it?'

'Oh, certainly.'

'If we ask them questions about their father, they'll have to answer?'

'If they're relevant, yes.'

'What d'you mean by "relevant?" '

'Something to do with the case.'

'Well, anything to do with the major is to do with the case, isn't it?'

'Not necessarily. What are those questions you want to ask of the sons?'

'Plenty of time for that. Blinkers, Mr Dealtry. Oh – I'm so sorry. You don't like the expression.' And Mr Trotter left Mr Dealtry on the steps of the County Court.

Mr Dealtry was now starting to come to the conclusion that his client might after all be a lunatic, even if not certifiable as one. Meanwhile, the major's opinion of the law had certainly improved and he had nothing but praise for Jane.

'Well, it's very nice of you, Major Buttonstep,' she said, 'but I really had nothing to do. I just left it to the registrar.'

'You don't weigh words by quantity, my dear,' he replied. 'You used few words, but always the right ones and at the right time. I hope your sister's as good as you are. What date did you say the trial will be?'

A few days later Mr Dealtry asked Jane whether, if he could persuade his client to agree to the major's original suggestion for a settlement, the offer was still open. Since the hearing, Mr Dealtry had arranged a conference with Mr Larpent. Mr Trotter had attended it and had appeared to be influenced by Mr Larpent's words of warning. Although he had spoken jauntily after the application before the registrar, Mr Larpent's advice, following swiftly on the registrar's reaction to the whole affair, appeared to have had its effect. He did not say definitely that he would agree, but instructed Mr Dealtry to find out whether the plaintiff would settle on the same terms.

'Certainly not,' said the major, when Jane told him the good news. 'He wanted a fight, he shall have one.'

The major had tasted blood. He had to admit to himself and his wife that it was not unpleasant.

CHAPTER ELEVEN

Apology for a Judge

His Honour Judge Smoothe, who was the judge of the Copplestone County Court, was very different from his registrar. For one thing he was much quieter. He was not by any means the quietest of all the judges but, unless provoked by counsel, he managed to maintain a reasonable degree of silence.

In countries where there is a separate profession of judges and they are not selected from advocates, it is natural that the average judge should by training have that particular quality. But in a country such as England, where every judge has been an advocate, often an outstanding one, it is perhaps rather surprising that so many of them are able to keep silent from the moment they get on the Bench. Up till that moment they have been accustomed to intervene whenever a chink in their opponent's armour appeared, and one would have supposed that this so conditioned them into a readiness to intervene that they would be unable to shake off the habit. One would not have expected the fact that they no longer cared which side won to be enough to prevent them from asking a question when, for example, they heard counsel cross-examining a witness in an inept manner. At the Bar *they* would have made mincemeat of the witness – whereas he is almost being let off altogether. One would have expected them to be unable to resist using their professional skill on the witness. It is quite true that, when both sides have asked all the questions which they wish to ask, a judge may ask a few very important pertinent questions, but it is a little surprising that the average judge is prepared to wait to do this. He is not like the ambitious schoolboy who, knowing the answer to a question, cannot refrain from putting up an eager hand, or even saying: 'please, sir, I know, sir.'

There are, of course, a few judges who do behave like the schoolboy and who cannot resist the temptation to intervene, but they form the minority and Judge Smoothe was not one of them. He had practised at the Bar in the days when there was, for the most part, a lower standard of County Court judge than there is today. And he learned a lot from such experiences. He had appeared before the rough-and-ready, the over-technical, the talkative, the too-silent judges (who said so little that advocates could not tell how their minds were working and could not, therefore, be certain to address their arguments to points which were troubling the judge), the over-anxious, the judges who never sat after lunch if they could avoid it, the sarcastic, the too-kindly judges who were prepared to put their hands in richer people's pockets to pay poorer people, whatever the merits might be, and so on.

Judge Smoothe was not a perfect judge, but he was observant and had made up his mind long before he was a judge that, if ever he were made one, he would not behave as some of them behaved. He was appalled, for example, at the way in which one judge, Judge Mountain, treated litigants in person. Judge Mountain knew a good deal about the technicalities of litigation and he was a fairly good lawyer, but he appeared to have no interest whatever in the merits of the cases he tried. He existed in the days before free legal aid could be obtained and if, for example, a woman who could not afford to employ a lawyer and was too nervous to state her case came before him, he would calmly dismiss her claim without going into its merits. It was up to her to prove her case, and if, through fear, illiteracy or complete ignorance of law and Court procedure or a combination of all these reasons, she did not give or call the necessary evidence, that was the end of the matter.

'Is that all you have to say, ma'am?' he would ask.

The wretched woman would stand quavering in the witness box and at the best would be able to stammer out 'Yes.'

'Case dismissed,' Judge Mountain would say and the plaintiff, who was owed rent by her tenant or was entitled to possession of the premises she had let or had some other righteous complaint against the defendant, would leave the Court without the slightest idea of what had happened.

It would indeed have been interesting to have seen Judge Mountain going through purgatory. Like most people who abuse the power vested in them, he would probably have been extremely apprehensive of the treatment which he was likely to receive. He might well have pictured the tormentors of the Middle Ages or other horrors. Perhaps what happened was something like this: 'Come in and sit down, your Honour, please,' said a gentle voice, and the judge walked in. No one was to be seen.

'Quite comfortable?' asked the voice.

The judge managed to say: 'Yes, thank you.'

'Good,' said the voice.

Although this was very different from the rough handling which he had expected, in a way it made him even more apprehensive of what was to come. Perhaps, he thought, it's deliberately done in order to make the torture feel worse when it actually starts. Or perhaps it's done as the torture itself, like the seconds which pass before the axe falls on the prisoner's neck. Whatever the reason for the mildness of the voice and the absence of torturers and instruments of torture, sweat started to gather on his forehead.

'Well, your Honour,' said the voice, 'shall we begin?'

'If you please,' said the judge.

'Do you know why you are here?'

'To purge my sins.'

'Then you sinned on earth?'

'All men do.'

'This suggests to me, your Honour, that you consider that your only sin was to be a man. To reduce it to syllogistic form, you say: "All men sin. I am a man. Therefore, I sin." But I expect you say to yourself that, for the life of you, you can't think of any particular sin you committed.'

'Indeed I can. I have committed the usual sin of selfishness.'

'Again, you seem to be trying to excuse yourself because many other people are also selfish. You said the "usual" sin of selfishness.'

'I see the point. I admit I have often been selfish.'

'Is that the worst you can say against yourself?'

The judge thought for a moment. They must know everything down here, he thought, there's no point in concealment.

'When I was a small boy I once stole a toy pistol from a shop. I tried to repay the money anonymously many years later, but the shop was no longer there.'

'Well, that's a start. What about in later years? What's the worst you can say about yourself?'

'I suppose I took too much pride in my personal appearance.'

'That's the worst you can say?'

'I am no judge of sin. I have committed the normal sin of thoughtlessness. As I've said, I was selfish. I was, I suppose, a little vain. Which is the worst of these sins I really don't know.'

'If I may respectfully say so, your Honour,' said the voice, 'your difficulty is that you don't seem to know a sin when you see one. How long were you a judge?'

'Just over fifteen years.'

'Your judicial life was one long sin.'

'Is it a sin then to be a judge? You mean that to presume to judge one's fellow creatures is in itself sinful?'

'It depends how you judge them.'

'I did my best according to my lights. I was not often upset in the Appeal Court.'

'I congratulate you, your Honour. No doubt that was a great satisfaction to you.'

'Yes, it was. I sinned there, I suppose. I should not have been so pleased. It was my duty to try the case properly.'

'Just look at that wall, please, your Honour.'

The judge turned his head and saw nothing but a white wall. A moment later a picture appeared on it – his Court.

'That's how it was when you presided.'

The judge looked at it with interest.

'As a matter of fact it hasn't changed since then. But this was taken when you were there. Watch.'

A woman came out of the Court crying.

'Can you think why she's crying, your Honour?'

'Women often cry. Perhaps she lost a case.'

'Before you?'

'Perhaps. It might have been before the registrar.'

'Did you often make your litigants cry?'

the same strictness to everyone. I know they didn't like it. I have had counsel get up and walk out of my Court because he didn't like the way I treated him. I have had companies move their registered offices so that their cases wouldn't be tried by me. I am aware that the staff at my Court did not like me, and that, for example, they would describe my preparing myself to make a dignified entrance into my Court as "scenting himself up." I could sense that I was unpopular with nearly every class of litigant. If a litigant in person could not prove the due service of an effective notice to quit, he lost his case for possession – even if the reason was that he had not kept a copy and did not remember what was in it. If you call this sin, every government department sins. You can't get a passport unless you fill in the correct form. You try putting on the back of a passport photograph "I certify this to be a rotten likeness." The person who brought it to you to sign will very likely say so himself – particularly herself: "It's terrible, isn't it?" she'll say. But she won't thank you for putting that on the back, because she'll get no passport. You try to get a driving licence without saying you've read the Highway Code. Fortunately they don't cross-examine people about that statement. But you'll get no licence unless you say you've read it. And you say I sinned because I was technical. Suppose I had gone the other way about it? "Now, Mrs Briggs, I'll tell you what you must do to win your case." What would Mrs Griggs on the other side have thought? I can't make them both win, can I? And what about the second-rate solicitor and counsel? Have I got to do all their work for them? I tell you this – a lot of advocates in my Court learned a great deal from appearing in front of me. Unless they wanted to make fools of themselves, they had to learn the rules before they came in front of me. If every judge had behaved like I did, it would

have raised the standard of advocacy all round and that
would have helped the litigants. And as for my treatment
of litigants in person, didn't that perhaps accelerate the
passing of the Legal Aid and Advice Act? If every litigant
had been nursed and coddled by me, there wouldn't have
been half the complaints about injustice, and you might
never have had free legal aid at all. I'll warrant that there
were plenty of complaints about me. You don't get
reforms until people cry out for them. I made them cry
out. Was that a sin? I took no judicial oath when I was
appointed. County Court judges didn't in those days. But
I venture to think that I fulfilled the terms of the oath
quite as well as those who do. I tried all my cases without
fear or favour, affection or ill-will. I'm not saying there
wasn't fear among those who appeared before me. There
was certainly ill-will. But none on my part. I feared no
one, I favoured no one. I liked no one, I disliked no one.
My court was clean of cant and loose talk. "Make up your
mind and formulate your proposition," I would say. I
forced them to think or at any rate to use what brains they
had. "That puts me in a difficulty, your Honour," an
advocate would say. "Difficulties were made to be
overcome," I would reply. Besides I was often asked
officially for my opinion on questions relating to the
practice in the Courts. Was that because my behaviour was
disapproved by the authorities? Of course there shouldn't
be any rules and there should be only one law. "Do right
to everyone." But in this imperfect world it wouldn't work.
And if you have rules, they must be observed. I'm not
saying I was a great judge. I wasn't. I would agree that I was
rather more suited for the High Court, where the standard
of advocacy is higher and there are hardly any litigants in
person. No, I have nothing to apologise for in my judicial
behaviour. Of course injustice was done in my Court. So it

CHAPTER TWELVE

Mr Larpent Opens

On the appointed day the case of *Buttonstep v Trotter* came before Judge Smoothe. The court was crowded, as local interest was considerable, and, as it proceeded, it even found its way into *The Times* – which reported it under the heading of 'The Major and the Mower.'

As soon as the case had been called by the clerk, Prunella rose and, after stating that she appeared for the plaintiff and that Mr Larpent appeared for the defendant, she submitted that the burden of proof was on Mr Trotter.

'The admissions made before the learned registrar,' she said, 'amount in my respectful submission *prima facie* to an admission of the claim. That being so, it is for the defendant to disprove liability if he can.'

'What d'you say to that, Mr Larpent?' asked the judge.

'Your Honour,' said Mr Larpent, 'if my learned friend will forgive my crossing swords with her on this particular issue, I would say this. All that was admitted before the learned registrar – and may I say at once that no criticism of any kind is made by me or by my client about the learned registrar, whom we all know if I may respectfully say so, to do his work with great care and skill, if that is not an impertinence – all that was admitted before the learned registrar was a demand and a *failure* to return, not a refusal. If I may take an extreme case. Suppose your Honour had borrowed an article from a friend and the friend came to collect it and asked your Honour for it but your Honour was unable to return it because you were dead, would that be detinue? I venture to submit not. But may I at once add that that was merely an example and that we all hope – for my part most profoundly – that your Honour will live to grace the Bench – if I may respectfully say so – for many a long day? But to that my learned friend with her usual acumen, if I may say so, may reply: "But death makes a difference." Well, we all know that it does, if I may say so, make a considerable difference. But suppose your Honour were just asleep and did not hear, or suppose you were ill and, though you heard the request, you could not comply with it – however much you wanted to – and I'm sure that in your Honour's case, if I may respectfully say so, you would want to – surely that would not be detinue? There must not be simply a failure to deliver up but a refusal to do so.'

'May not a failure constitute a refusal?'

'Oh, your Honour is, if I may say so, as always perfectly right. But I have, I respectfully hope, demonstrated that a *mere* failure does not necessarily constitute a refusal. It is, in my very respectful submission, for the plaintiff to prove that the particular failure in this case did constitute a refusal. The only admission recorded by the learned registrar was a failure.'

'A failure at your client's own house where the mowing machine was at that moment,' said the judge.

'But the defendant may have been unable to move the machine owing to sickness, your Honour.'

'Wouldn't that be for him to prove, Mr Larpent? There is no qualification to the admission. Surely, as long as you admit that the plaintiff called for the article at your client's house and he failed to hand it over there and then, that is sufficient evidence of a demand and refusal – until you prove that he was physically incapable of handing over?'

'And, even then,' put in Prunella, prompted by Jane, 'he could have let my client in to fetch it.'

'I'm sure,' said Mr Larpent, 'that my learned friend did not intend to incommode me by interrupting, but I should be most grateful if she would reserve her remarks until I have finished.'

'I'm so sorry,' said Prunella.

'Not at all,' said Mr Larpent.

'There's something in the point though, isn't there, Mr Larpent?' said the judge. 'Not only is there no explanation so far why the defendant did not hand the machine over, but there is the fact that he did not invite the plaintiff in to take it away himself. Surely in that state of affairs there is abundant evidence of demand and refusal – unless and until your client gives some explanation to displace the natural inference from the admitted facts?'

'Well, your Honour,' said Mr Larpent, 'if your Honour – with all your Honour's experience, the benefit of which we in this Court have had and, if I may respectfully say so, I hope will have for a long time – if your Honour thinks that, although I must respectfully reserve the point, your Honour will understand what I mean and knows me well enough, I am sure, to understand that I intend no impertinence to your Honour in keeping the point open just in case there should happen to be an appeal against your Honour's judgment ...'

'It might be in your favour, Mr Larpent,' the judge could not resist saying. 'I haven't heard the case yet.'

'Oh, of course, your Honour, in those circumstances I should not advise my client to appeal. And, indeed, at this early stage I did not intend for a moment to imply that there was likely to be an appeal – whatever the result of the case – I just wanted very respectfully to keep the point open – in all those circumstances then I will accept your Honour's decision on the point – subject, of course, to my reserving my client's rights in the matter as I respectfully hope I have sufficiently explained – and I will accept that the burden of proof is on my client.'

'Very well, Mr Larpent, then you begin,' said the judge.

'If your Honour pleases. The claim in this case is, if I may say so, a very simple one. The plaintiff lent the defendant a mowing machine. The defendant did not return it, in spite of the plaintiff's demands and the plaintiff now brings this action for its return. The only issue on this part of the case is whether the defendant actually refused to return it.'

'Has he returned it now?' asked the judge.

'He has not, your Honour, and, while your Honour may – I only say may – come to the conclusion that he ought to have done so, I will explain to your Honour why he has not. But, first, I wish to point out very respectfully that the only question your Honour has to try is whether, at the time of the issue of the summons – I repeat, at the time of the issue of the summons – there had been a demand and a refusal.'

'I don't usually intervene at this stage,' said the judge, 'but, as this is admittedly the plaintiff's mower, it seems rather hard on him that he should be deprived of its use at a time when he needs it most.'

'May I respectfully agree,' said Mr Larpent, 'but there is a reason. It is all bound up, if I may say so, with the counterclaim. Suppose, for example, your Honour should award damages exceeding the value of the mower to the defendant, he will have at any rate some security for your

Honour's order and would have property on which he could levy execution.'

'Is there any reason to think that Major Buttonstep could not or would not pay any damages awarded against him?'

'I can't say, your Honour, but I can say that there is a great deal of bitterness between the parties about this matter. Otherwise, indeed, your Honour would never have been troubled with it.'

'I see,' said the judge. 'A quarrel between neighbours.'

'Oddly enough,' said Mr Larpent, 'although the parties are in fact near neighbours, they did not know each other before this trouble began. Mr Trotter has only just come to Buttonstep. Major Buttonstep has, I believe – I speak subject to correction by my learned friend – lived there all his life. My learned friend does not, I perceive, correct me. So, your Honour can take that as a fact. So much for the claim. The facts are in a very small compass and, if I may say so, will not cause your Honour much trouble. Now for the counterclaim which, I venture to say, is the nub of the matter. Major Buttonstep, on failing to obtain his mower back from the defendant, went to see PC Glossop, whom I shall call before your Honour, and it was in the officer's presence that he made what I think I may say without exaggeration are very serious imputations on the defendant's character. He said and repeated twice – I call your Honour's attention to that matter – it was not just the case of a man saying something quickly in a temper – he repeated twice that my client was either mad or that he had stolen the machine. Now, I hope I am not one of those advocates, your Honour, who call every case "the most serious case of which I've heard," or say of every slander "I cannot think of anything more grave that the plaintiff could have said." He could, for example, have called my client a murderer or a blackmailer, he could have said he was a robber of offertory boxes, that he kidnapped children or was trying to poison his wife. He did none of these things. He said he had stolen a mowing machine or was mad. But, although the plaintiff might have said something worse of my client, I submit, with very considerable confidence, if I may say so, that what he said was serious enough, that it was indeed a gross slander. Not the gravest possible by any means, but none the less grave. And he published it, your Honour will note this, he published it to the village constable. Now, if I were the type of advocate who indulged in the sort of hyperboles to which I have referred, I might well have said: "Could he have published on a more grievous occasion from the defendant's point of view?" But, even though I am not an advocate of that type, I venture to say that I should not have been far out if I had asked that question. Here is my client in an entirely new neighbourhood, unknown to anyone, desirous of getting on with his neighbours ...'

'He showed a queer way of starting,' said Prunella.

'Now, really,' said Mr Larpent. 'My learned friend must not take advantage of the fact that she is greatly admired by all the members of the Bar – including myself – to make such unwarrantable interruptions.'

'I thought it was most apt,' whispered the major to Digby.

'I was saying,' went on Mr Larpent, 'when my learned friend, if I may say so without offence, forgot herself, I was saying that here was my client, anxious to be held in good regard all round – and what happens? The plaintiff says to the village policeman: "He's mad or he stole." A lie goes round the world, it has been said, while truth is putting her boots on. And, if I may add to the quotation, it travels fast round the world. Do you think that Mrs Temperley, who keeps the village post office and store, would not soon hear about it? What credit will the plaintiff get at her shop? He may be honest but, if so, he is mad. Lunatics are not the best customers. But he may be sane. If so, he is a thief. No credit for him. And what about the local inn where he may wish to repair for a quick drink? Can't your Honour see the nudges and the looks, and hear the whispers as he comes in? Won't the landlord make sure he has his money before he hands over the pint?'

'Forgive me, Mr Larpent,' said the judge, 'but every landlord ought to do that if he wants to be sure of his money. An innkeeper cannot sue for a debt in respect of beer, cider or perry to be consumed on the premises.'

'That's my point, your Honour. In most cases a landlord will be prepared to take a risk. If I go into a public house and order some beer I hope I can say that most landlords would hand it to me before I paid for it. But, if they thought I was mad or a thief, would they take that risk? Surely not. How embarrassing for my client when everyone sees the landlord holding tightly on to the tankard until the money is put on to the counter and perhaps even then only releases the drink when he has taken the money with his other hand. Meanwhile, the other people in the bar are giving him sidelong glances. And all this to a man who is neither mad nor a thief. Perhaps I should have told your Honour that the plaintiff does not attempt to justify his allegations. He admits that there is no truth whatever in his assertions. Although he made those wicked allegations three times – I respectfully submit that wicked is not too strong a term to use – he now calmly admits that my client is neither mad nor bad.'

'And what is the defence to the claim for slander?'

'Only privilege, your Honour. Publication is admitted. Justification is not alleged. The plaintiff hides behind the plea of privilege.'

'I don't see why you should scoff at the plea, Mr Larpent. It is a perfectly proper plea. If a man has a duty or a right to say something to a person and he believes in the truth of what he says he ought not to be liable to an action for slander. That's all the plea of privilege amounts to. Otherwise one could seldom give a genuine reference in which some criticism was made of the person concerned.'

'I respectfully agree, your Honour. I wasn't intending to suggest for a moment that the plea of privilege was not a perfectly proper plea. But, in order to establish it, the plaintiff must prove that he believed that what he said was true – namely that my client was either mad or was a thief.'

'Not a thief in general,' said Prunella, again prompted by Jane. 'Just a man who stole my client's mowing machine.'

'Well, that's a thief,' said Mr Larpent, 'with great respect.'

'Your Honour,' said Prunella, 'when one talks of a thief, the average person means a person who is either known as a thief or regularly steals things. My client does not suggest and never has suggested that the defendant is a thief in that sense of the word. All he said was that the defendant had either stolen his mowing machine or that he was mad. And, if it's any help to my friend, my client still thinks so. He will say that the defendant's conduct was calculated to make any sane person believe that those were the only alternatives.'

The usually mild Mr Larpent sat down with a bump – so hard in fact that it jarred his spine and he wished he hadn't. His gesture was to indicate to Prunella that he strongly resented her intervention and was an accepted method of indicating to an opponent that, if he or she has a proper objection to make, it had better be made and, if not, he or she had better shut up. As Prunella also sat down at the same time, but without any emphasis, and Mr Larpent was nursing his painful back, the judge was left with no one addressing him.

'I suppose,' he said rather plaintively after a moment or two, 'that someone is going to talk to me?'

Mr Larpent recovered himself and jumped up.

'I'm so extremely sorry, your Honour. I do apologise. I thought my learned friend had some objection to make. If at any time I mis-state the facts or do anything I should not – and I hope your Honour knows me well enough to be sure that I should never do such a thing on purpose – should that happen, I should welcome an intervention by my learned friend to put me right – we are all fallible, your Honour, at least I certainly am – and I do not suggest that some interventions cannot properly be made. But I must admit, if I may say so without being offensive to my learned friend, that I do most strongly resent interjections by her which are not prompted by any mistake made by me but simply by a desire on her part to say something to forward her case at a time when it is my right – and I may say duty – to put forward my client's submissions on the matter to the best of my ability. No doubt what my learned friend said was relevant and proper but it was quite unnecessary to say it when she did and, without intending to hurt her feelings, I must say that I shall be most obliged if she will refrain from interrupting unless, as I indicated before, I make some error.'

'You did make an error,' said Prunella. 'You said that my client called your client a thief. He did not. He said that he had stolen his mowing machine – if he was not mad.'

'I repeat,' said Mr Larpent, 'that that is an allegation of theft.'

'Yes, Mr Larpent,' said the judge, 'but of a single theft, not wholesale or regular thieving. I think Miss Coombe is right in saying that most people would understand the expression "the man is a thief" in a general sense and not to imply that on one occasion he had stolen one article.'

'If your Honour pleases,' said Mr Larpent. 'Let it be made plain then that the defendant does not suggest that the plaintiff was saying to the constable anything more than that the defendant had stolen the plaintiff's mowing machine.'

'Unless he was mad,' put in Prunella.

'I'm obliged to my learned friend,' said Mr Larpent. 'Exactly so, unless he was mad. It's a nice alternative, isn't it, your Honour, if I may ask a rhetorical question? Either mad or a stealer of mowing machines.'

'One mowing machine,' said Prunella, 'the plaintiff's mowing machine.'

'My learned friend is perfectly right,' said Mr Larpent. 'I'm obliged for the correction. One mowing machine. The plaintiff's mowing machine. That's a nice thing to say about a person who has just come to the neighbourhood. But, your Honour, the matter doesn't stop there. It doesn't stop there by a long way. When my learned friend's client first made this opprobrious suggestion about my client, he was invited by my client to apologise. That seemed a most reasonable attitude, if I may say so, on the part of my client. Thinking that the words might have been said in the heat of the moment or without a realisation of their gravity, the defendant asked the plaintiff to apologise. And what was the result? What was the result?'

Mr Larpent paused to give dramatic effect. So long in fact that the judge said: 'Well, what was it, Mr Larpent? There's no jury, you know, to be influenced by your rhetorical powers, effective as they are.'

'Oh, your Honour,' said Mr Larpent almost abjectly, 'I wouldn't dream of treating your Honour like a jury. I do hope that your Honour doesn't think that I would do a thing like that. If I have erred I do most strongly crave your Honour's indulgence.'

'That's all right, Mr Larpent,' said the judge. 'All I couldn't understand was why you repeated the question, and why you paused.'

'I'm afraid it was habit, your Honour,' said Mr Larpent. 'I'm afraid that after some years at the Bar one forms these habits, and I do most humbly apologise to your Honour if I have given you the slightest impression that I thought I was addressing a jury.'

'Oh, well, Mr Larpent,' said the judge, 'juries aren't as bad as all that, you know.'

'Certainly not,' said Mr Larpent, 'they're very good.'

'Then why apologise for treating me as one?'

'Oh, your Honour understands, I'm sure, what I mean. Juries are good, very good indeed – they are the mainstay of a democratic way of life, but judges are so much better, your Honour.'

'I'm not so sure, Mr Larpent, that it wouldn't have been much better for a jury to try this action. You could have had one, you know.'

'I preferred and I think that here for once, if I may say so, I can speak for my learned friend – we both preferred to have your Honour. For one thing, it's so much quicker.'

'Perhaps it is,' said the judge, 'but, if I may say so, you seem to be addressing me in much the same manner and at much the same length as though I were a jury. Don't think I mind, Mr Larpent. I'm enjoying listening to you. But, as you talked of saving time, I thought I'd just mention it.'

'Please forgive me, your Honour,' said Mr Larpent. 'If I have erred, it is from zeal. I felt that, as slander actions are rarely tried in your Honour's court, I ought to open this case at rather greater length than usual. I'm sure your Honour will check me if I go on too long.'

'I have,' said the judge gently.

'Quite so,' said Mr Larpent, 'and I'm most grateful to your Honour for reminding me, if I may say so, that the hands of the clock are turning. But, as this is a slander action, I think I should put your Honour in full possession of the facts before I call the evidence. I think I was talking, your Honour, of the defendant's reaction when the plaintiff first made the statement complained of. He asked for an apology. And what was the result. What was ...'

With an effort Mr Larpent checked himself from repeating the question.

'The plaintiff, instead of apologising, repeated the allegation. And, as if that weren't enough, he said it again. Now, your Honour, granted that the first time he said the words they were said in anger without proper thought – I don't admit that that was the case – far from it – but just suppose for the sake of argument that they were – what shall we say about the second and third repetitions? What about them? The plaintiff had been reminded of the gravity of what he was saying. He had been asked to apologise. And what does he do? What does ... So far from apologising he deliberately – and that is the nub of the matter, your Honour – he deliberately says them again. Those are not words spoken hastily in the heat of the moment. There speaks the slanderer determined to traduce my client. Not twice, but three times. This is not an angry unmeant phrase, but a deliberate slander.'

'I don't quite understand, Mr Larpent,' said the judge. 'Are you saying that the plaintiff was not angry when he repeated the words?'

'That will be my submission, your Honour.'

'Well, isn't that worse for your client, not better? If the plaintiff was angry all the time it might be difficult to satisfy a Court that he really thought about what he was saying. And, as he now admits the words weren't true but has to prove that he believed them to be true, isn't it much more difficult for him to prove that, if he was in a temper all the time. What does an angry man really believe? Does he really think what he's saying? And, if he doesn't, how can he believe it to be true? But if the plaintiff, after weighing up your client's conduct in failing to return the mowing machine after several demands had been made, says quite deliberately, probably first to himself and later to the constable: "this man either intends to steal the machine or he must be mad," is it not easier for him to prove that at the time he spoke the words he really believed them?'

Mr Larpent spoke to his solicitor who in turn spoke to Mr Trotter.

'Will your Honour forgive me a moment?' said Mr Larpent, 'while I take instructions.'

A few moments later – after a hasty conversation with Mr Dealtry, Mr Larpent went on: 'I'm most grateful to your Honour for giving me that opportunity. Your Honour is, as always, perfectly right. There is no question but that, when the words were repeated, Major Buttonstep was still angry.'

'Then the repetition of the alleged slander was made in the heat of the moment?' asked the judge. 'Is that your case?'

'Your Honour puts me in a difficulty,' said Mr Larpent.

'I don't see why,' said the judge, 'unless you want to have it both ways.'

'I'd prefer to see how it turns out in the evidence, your Honour, before committing myself.'

'That's what I call having it both ways,' said the judge.

'Not both ways, your Honour. Just wanting to see which way.'

'The cat will jump,' whispered Jane to Prunella.

'Now really,' said Mr Larpent, 'I do most strongly object to *sotto voce* remarks being made by my learned friend's solicitor to her.'

'I heard nothing,' said the judge, 'but how otherwise can Miss Coombe be instructed during the progress of the case?'

'Oh, your Honour,' said Mr Larpent, 'I should have no objection at all – indeed, I could have no objection, if I may say so, to my learned friend's client instructing her – but these were not instructions, your Honour. It was a gibe or quip, and it's very difficult to conduct a case if there's going to be a muffled accompaniment of gibes or quips between my learned friend and her client.'

'I apologise to my learned friend,' said Prunella.

'I'm very much obliged,' said Mr Larpent. 'I think we can now say that the incident is closed, if I may put it in that way.'

'Now how d'you put your client's case?' asked the judge. 'Are you saying that the slanders were spoken in the heat of the moment or not?'

'I hope I shall not incur your Honour's displeasure if I leave the evidence to speak for itself.'

'I hope it will speak fairly soon,' said the judge. 'I shouldn't have asked the question if you hadn't been speaking so much on behalf of the evidence.'

'I do hope your Honour does not think that I'm opening this case at too great a length,' said Mr Larpent.

'Well as you ask me, I do, as a matter of fact,' replied the judge. 'While it's always delightful to listen to you, Mr Larpent, I want to hear what the witnesses say.'

'Your Honour is always exceptionally kind. Then I won't detain your Honour a moment longer, except to say that, from the moment these slanders were published until now, there has not been – I won't say an apology – not a hint of an apology from the plaintiff. I submit that, if he had not been actuated by malice when he spoke the words – whether spoken in heat or not – he would later on, as soon as he discovered that they were untrue, have apologised for them – just as my learned friend apologised to me a few moments ago. That's what the normal person, who is not actuated by malice, does as soon as he or she discovers the mistake. But not so the plaintiff. Oh dear no. Not a word of apology or withdrawal. Did he write a letter to Constable Glossop and say that my client had not stolen the machine and was not mad? No, he did not. I ask myself – why not? I ask your Honour why not. Why not, I repeat.'

'I wish you wouldn't,' said the judge. 'I got the point the first time.'

'I'm so sorry, your Honour. I hope your Honour will overlook the many deficiencies in my presentation of the defendant's case. The fact is, your Honour, that the case is an extremely important one from his point of view, and I find the responsibility of ensuring that I overlook nothing which can be said upon his behalf a very heavy one. New to the neighbourhood, a stranger ... '

'Really, Mr Larpent, you made it abundantly plain what seems a long time ago that the defendant was new to the neighbourhood.'

'I'm so sorry, your Honour. It's so difficult for an advocate to know what facts are retained in the learned judge's mind and what are not. I know how carefully your Honour listens to everything but, nevertheless, it might be that some small point might have escaped your Honour's notice.'

'Look, Mr Larpent, let's see if anything has escaped my notice. As far as I can see the facts in this case can be stated in about fifty words. The defendant, a newcomer to Buttonstep, borrows the plaintiff's mowing machine. Although repeatedly asked to return it he does not do so. The plaintiff calls in the village constable and in his presence states that the defendant is either mad or has stolen the plaintiff's machine. The plaintiff has not apologised for this statement. That's all, isn't it? That probably took me about twenty seconds to say. You've been going for twenty minutes.'

'But, your Honour,' said Mr Larpent, 'we have not all your Honour's gift for succinctness or for picking out the salient points in a case.'

'Well, now that I've picked them out, is there anything else you want to say before calling the evidence?'

'Only this, your Honour. It is with very great regret that the defendant is taking part in these proceedings. He had hoped, when he came to the neighbourhood, that he would live in amity with his neighbours, and he realises to the full that an action in the County Court is not the best start. But what was he to do, your Honour? What was he to do?'

'Well,' said the judge, 'he could have handed back the machine, for one thing.'

'And be branded a lunatic, your Honour, or admit he had stolen the machine? I ask rhetorically – I know I mustn't ask your Honour questions – however kind your

Honour may be sometimes in answering them – I ask rhetorically, what could he do but take proceedings to protect his good name? His good name, your Honour. Something which all of us hold more dear to us than ...'

Mr Larpent paused. The judge's attention appeared to have wandered and he was looking fixedly at the empty jury box.

'Go on, Mr Larpent, go on,' he said after the pause had become too long. 'There's no one there to hear you, but pray go on. Tell them that who steals your purse (or your mowing machine, for that matter) steals trash. 'Twas mine, 'tis his and has been slave to thousands. I'm sure they'd be most affected.'

'I was going to say that, as a matter of fact, your Honour. Is there anything wrong about it? But he that filches from me my good name ...'

'I know it, Mr Larpent, I know it all. I used to recite it long before you took your Bar examinations.'

'I'm so sorry, your Honour. In other words, however foolish the defendant may have been about the mowing machine, the plaintiff did worse by stealing not a trumpery thing like a mowing machine but one of the essentials to happiness – his good name. The plaintiff is an old established and, I dare say, respected resident of the neighbourhood. He no doubt has a reputation which could withstand an imputation or two. But my unfortunate client has no goodwill in the neighbourhood at all. Who could be more vulnerable to a slanderous attack? There is only one way in which my client can – I was going to say re-establish himself in the area – but it should be establish himself there, and that is by obtaining heavy damages at your Honour's hands, damages which will establish once and for all – first, that my client's integrity and sanity are unquestioned and, secondly, that the plaintiff spoke out of malice, out of a desire to hurt my client. Before I call the evidence, your Honour …'

'Really,' said the judge, 'it's about ten minutes since you assured me you had only "this" to say before you called the witnesses. You have not only said "this" but you have gone on to "that" and "the other" and, if I'm not very much mistaken, you will shortly be going back to "this".'

'I do hope I'm not wearying your Honour.'

'Well, if you ask me, you are, Mr Larpent. I'm sure it's not only I who want to get on with the case, but the plaintiff and the defendant too. No doubt what you say is all very proper and relevant, but I'm fully in possession of the necessary facts to enable me to listen to the evidence with a full knowledge of what the points at issue are. You know, Mr Larpent, there are some judges who would never have allowed you to go on like this.'

'I'm most grateful to your Honour for allowing me to continue. I have almost finished my opening address. After all, I have another speech later.'

'You have indeed,' said the judge sorrowfully. 'I was hoping to reach it today.'

'Well, your Honour, I will reserve what I can of my remarks until my closing speech. Suffice it to say, for the moment, that, although my client is coming here in the guise of a defendant, he is really the plaintiff. And, indeed, nothing could demonstrate that more clearly than the fact that it is I who am opening the case and not my learned opponent.'

'You tried hard to make me open it,' said Prunella.

'Please, Miss Coombe,' said the judge. 'Please keep quite quiet, and, if I can do so too, Mr Larpent may eventually call the evidence.'

'I am obliged to my learned friend for reminding me of that matter,' said Mr Larpent.

'I told you so,' said the judge, looking at Prunella.

'I beg your Honour's pardon?' said Mr Larpent.

'Nothing,' said the judge. 'Please go on.'

'I was saying,' said Mr Larpent, 'that I was very much indebted to my learned friend for reminding me that my client is technically a defendant, but what I want to point out to your Honour is that, though in a sense the mowing machine has something to do with the slander, the claim for slander is really an independent action and could have been brought as such – not, it is true, in this Court but in the High Court. Indeed, it was a considerable question for my client's advisers whether to issue separate proceedings there or to counterclaim in this Court. Eventually, out of mercy to the plaintiff, my client decided to make his claim in this action.'

'If there's any mercy about,' whispered the judge to himself, 'I wish he'd have it on me.'

'So I hope your Honour will bear in mind, when you come to deal with the slander action, that it is entirely due to the meritorious action of the defendant in failing to take separate proceedings in the High Court that the matter is before your Honour at all.'

'I'm beginning to wish he had taken separate proceedings in the High Court,' said the judge, who could no longer keep his thoughts to a whisper.

Prunella looked at the judge as sympathetically as she thought was proper.

'But in that case,' said Mr Larpent, 'there would have been two sets of costs instead of one and, apart from the expense, there would have been much delay and considerable inconvenience for the parties. So, your Honour, my client is really the plaintiff in the slander action, and he asks you by your judgment to put an end once and for all to any rumours which may have been put into circulation by reason of these false statements.'

Mr Larpent paused. The judge sighed. At last, he thought to himself, we're coming to the evidence.

'That is all I wish to say to your Honour about the facts.'

Good, thought the judge. Now we can begin.

'As to the law,' went on Mr Larpent, 'I have brought a number of authorities which may interest your Honour,' and he brought out from under the desk seven or eight books bound together with a strap.

'I don't know if it would be convenient for your Honour to consider them now?'

'What point of law arises?'

'That depends, your Honour, but I think it possible that, as few slander actions are tried in the County Court, your Honour might care for me to refresh your Honour's memory, if I may respectfully put it that way, with the main ingredients of this cause of action.'

'If you simply wish to deliver a lecture on the law of slander, Mr Larpent,' said the judge, 'I need not trouble you. No doubt the Council of Legal Education would be grateful for any offers you care to make to them.'

'Oh, your Honour, I do hope your Honour doesn't think that I was implying ...'

'I do think, Mr Larpent, that that is exactly what you were implying.'

'Oh, your Honour, I do assure your Honour that I was only trying to be of such small assistance as I could be to your Honour. I would never venture to suggest that your Honour isn't far better acquainted with any aspect of the law than I am. It was just in case ...'

'If there is any particular point of law likely to arise in this case, by all means state what it is and refer me shortly – shortly, please, to the relevant authorities. If, however, it is impossible to tell whether any point will arise until the evidence has been heard, let us leave the law until we have heard the facts.'

'If your Honour pleases,' said Mr Larpent. 'Very well, then, I'll call the plaintiff, I mean the defendant.'

CHAPTER THIRTEEN

Evidence for the Defence

Mr Trotter, who had been getting stiffer and stiffer on the hard benches provided for litigants in most County Courts, was quite glad to get up and walk into the witness box. He took the oath, was asked his name and address, and was then questioned by Mr Larpent about the facts leading up to the borrowing of the mowing machine and the words spoken by the major in the presence of the constable.

Before Mr Larpent finished his examination-in-chief, he asked Mr Trotter: 'Where is the machine now?'

'In my garden.'

'Are you prepared to return it to the plaintiff?'

'Certainly.'

'When?'

'When he's paid me the damages which the judge orders.'

'In the event of the learned judge not awarding you damages, what then? You see, Mr Trotter, whatever you and I may think, it is at least theoretically possible, if I may say so, that your claim for slander will not succeed.'

'Why not?' asked Mr Trotter. 'I am not mad, I did not steal his mowing machine. It was slander to say I *was* one or *did* the other. Why shouldn't he pay for it?'

'That's for his Honour to say. The learned judge might, for example, I do not say for a moment he will, but the learned judge might say that the plaintiff was protected by what we lawyers call privilege.'

'Yes,' said Mr Trotter reminiscently, 'you did say something about that when I was in your chambers. Remind me, please.'

'Now, Mr Larpent and Mr Trotter,' intervened the judge, 'I am not prepared to listen to this conversation any longer. Mr Trotter, you were asked a perfectly proper question by your learned counsel, and a perfectly simple one. Kindly answer it.'

'I'm afraid I've forgotten it now,' said Mr Trotter.

'I'm not surprised,' said the judge. 'The question was – when will you hand over the machine if I do not award damages to you for slander?'

'But I've never considered such a possibility,' said Mr Trotter.

'Well, consider it now, please,' said the judge.

'What, here and now, standing in this witness box?'

'Certainly.'

'I don't think I could, your Honour. It's difficult enough to remember one's name and address when standing here, let alone tell a coherent story. My heart's beating like I don't know what. How can I really consider anything from here?'

'You may sit down, if you prefer it,' said the judge.

'But the seats are so uncomfortable,' complained Mr Trotter. 'I ache all over as it is.'

'Mr Trotter,' said the judge severely, 'if you are trying to be funny, you will get into very serious trouble. I'm not going to have this Court played about with.'

'I shouldn't dream of any such thing, your Honour,' said Mr Trotter, 'but you've frightened me more than ever now.

How I shall be able to continue my evidence I really don't know. You see, your Honour, I've never been in a Court before, let alone in a witness box, and I find it a very unnerving experience. My counsel and your Honour are used to it all, but I'm not. It's easy enough to forget things or get things wrong in ordinary conversation but I wonder everything didn't fly out of my head as soon as I took the oath. And now your Honour asks me to consider something, and warns me that I'll get into trouble if I don't. I suppose by "trouble" you mean you'll send me to prison. When I walked in here this morning I thought your Honour was looking at me and I was terrified that I might do something wrong and would be sent to prison before the case began. I'm sorry, your Honour, to have to talk like this but I don't think you and my counsel realise what it means to an ordinary chap like me to be brought here. I'm just an ordinary man who goes about his business ...'

'That will do, Mr Trotter,' said the judge.

'Who goes about his business in an ordinary way and ...'

'Be quiet, Mr Trotter,' said the judge. 'You are certainly not tongue-tied. But I do, as it happens, realise that witnesses may be very nervous and that in consequence their minds may go blank all of a sudden. Every judge does, and makes allowances accordingly. Occasionally people faint even. You can leave it to me to see that you are fully protected, and I will help you as far as it is proper for me to do so. Now, try to pull yourself together and answer this question: if you get no damages, when will you return the mowing machine?'

Mr Trotter hesitated for a few moments.

'Well?' asked the judge.

'My mind's gone blank,' said Mr Trotter.

'Now, look here,' began the judge sternly.

'Now you're threatening me again,' said Mr Trotter. 'It isn't easy for me, is it? First you threaten me and then you say you'll help me and then you threaten me again. Oh dear, I believe I feel faint.'

And Mr Trotter either swayed or gave a very creditable imitation of a person swaying.

'Let the witness have a chair,' said the judge, and the usher brought one and put it in the witness box. Mr Trotter turned round and looked at the chair with disfavour.

'I don't like the idea,' he said.

'Sit down, sir,' said the judge.

'Supposing it tips over,' asked Mr Trotter, 'who'll pay the damages?'

There was some sense in what Mr Trotter said, as the witness box was raised a few inches from the ground and was so small that the hind legs of the chair were only a fraction of an inch from the drop.

'Let the chair be placed outside the witness box,' said the judge, and this was done.

'I should remind you,' said Mr Larpent, 'that you are still on oath even though you're not actually in the witness box. I trust your Honour will forgive me for intervening, but I have known a witness who did not appreciate that fact.'

'Well, now,' said the judge, 'suppose we get on. If you don't get any damages, when will you return the machine?'

'Could I have a glass of water, please?' asked Mr Trotter.

The usher looked at the judge, the judge nodded, and a glass of water was produced for Mr Trotter. He drank it in sips, as some people would drink wine. When he had finished the judge said: 'Do you feel all right now?'

'No,' said Mr Trotter.

'What's the matter?'

'It's the atmosphere, your Honour.'

'Open some windows, please,' said the judge.

The usher, who was having quite a busy time, opened the windows.

'Is that better?' asked the judge.

'I didn't mean that kind of atmosphere,' said Mr Trotter. 'I meant the general atmosphere of the Court. As a matter of fact it's going to get a bit chilly with those windows open.'

The usher looked at the judge, who shook his head.

'Has your client been examined by a doctor for … for fainting fits or anything of that kind, Mr Larpent?' asked the judge.

'He's been thoroughly examined by two doctors, your Honour,' said Mr Larpent, 'who find that he is completely sane.'

'I didn't ask you that, Mr Larpent. I said "has he been examined for fainting fits?" '

'Not to my knowledge, your Honour.'

'I've never felt faint before,' said Mr Trotter, 'not till I came in here.'

'In my opinion,' said the judge, 'your client is perfectly able to answer questions but, if you wish to apply for an adjournment on the ground that he is not well enough to give evidence, I will hear your application and, if necessary, adjourn for a medical examination. And I hope you will make it clear to your client that, if in fact he is being impertinent, I shall not hesitate to use my powers under section – section …'

The judge picked up a green book and looked in it.

'I think your Honour means section 139,' said Mr Larpent helpfully.

'Thank you,' said the judge, and turned over some pages. 'The more important part of that seems to have been repealed,' he said.

'Oh – I'm sorry, your Honour.'

Mr Larpent picked up a similar green book and started to look through it feverishly. Prunella picked up hers and started to look at it, but less feverishly.

'This is odd,' said the judge. 'I can still fine under section 139, but the power of imprisonment appears to have been removed.'

Mr Trotter mouthed 'Good,' but the judge did not see it.

'Ah – no, I see. For some reason I'm given the power of imprisonment by section 29 of the 1956 Act, while the power of fining remains under section 139 of the 1934 Act. I wonder why it was done that way? There must have been a reason. However that may be, your client must remember that both powers exist.'

Mr Trotter looked glum and without saying a word showed by his face that he was thinking: 'There you go again – threatening me with prison.'

'Now, Mr Larpent, d'you wish to apply for an adjournment?'

'Might I consult my client first, please?' asked Mr Larpent.

'Certainly.'

Mr Larpent had a whispered conversation with Mr Trotter, and then said: 'No, your Honour. My client is perhaps rather more sensitive to the atmosphere of a court of law than many people are, but he will do his best to assist your Honour.'

'Very well, then,' said the judge. 'When will you hand back the machine if you get no damages?'

Mr Trotter apparently made a decision.

'Any time,' he said.

'Any time?'

'Well, during the hours of daylight. The plaintiff came for it about 2 a.m. once. It's hardly surprising he didn't get it.'

'Is that correct, Mr Larpent?' asked the judge in a slightly surprised voice.

'Certainly,' said Mr Larpent. 'My client can hardly be blamed for not giving it back at that time of night.'

'Is that what this case is about? Why didn't you tell me before, Mr Larpent?'

'Well, your Honour, if I may respectfully say so without impertinence your Honour did not exactly encourage me to prolong my opening and so I thought …'

'You said a great deal in your opening, Mr Larpent,' said the judge, 'some of it several times, or so it seemed, but at no time did you even hint at the fact that the reason for your client's failure to deliver up the machine was because the plaintiff came at a ridiculous time.'

'Get up,' whispered Jane to Prunella. 'Tell him.'

Up got Prunella.

'It was only after delivery had been refused several times at a normal time of day – one such time actually chosen by the defendant himself – that the plaintiff attempted to indulge in what I might describe as self help,' said Prunella.

'Oh, I see,' said the judge. 'Is that correct, Mr Larpent?'

'The plaintiff certainly tried to break into my client's premises at night and was dissuaded from pursuing the attempt by Constable Glossop.'

'Let's get on then,' said the judge. 'And let us get this plain, Mr Trotter. If you get no damages, you'll hand over the machine when it's called for at any time during the day by appointment?'

'I shall certainly advise my client to do so,' said Mr Larpent.

'I'm sure you would, Mr Larpent, but I want to be sure that your client would act on such advice. That's plain, is it, Mr Trotter?'

'Well,' said Mr Trotter, 'it's Major Buttonstep's mower and I really don't see why he shouldn't have it.'

'Thank you, Mr Trotter,' said Mr Larpent and sat down.

'No, don't go away,' he added, as Mr Trotter got up to go back to his seat in the court. 'My learned friend will want to ask you some questions.'

Mr Trotter sat down again and Prunella got up.

'Mr Trotter,' she began, 'has your behaviour in Court been a fair guide to your behaviour outside it?'

'By no means,' said Mr Trotter. 'You'll find me quite normal and ordinary outside Court, as I was telling his Honour. But I've got the jitters in here all right.'

'Have you ever had mumps?'

'Certainly not.'

'Did you not tell my client first that you had mumps in the house and then that you had them yourself?'

'I said something of the kind.'

'It was untrue?'

'Naturally.'

'Why did you tell my client an untruth?'

'I wanted to put him off.'

'Why?'

'It was not convenient to return the mower at that time.'

'Why didn't you say that instead of telling a lie?'

'Major Buttonstep's attitude was provocative. I'm quite a peaceable person unless I'm provoked, but then I may become awkward.'

'So you became awkward to Major Buttonstep?'

'I hope so.'

'Don't you think he might have mistaken your awkwardness for mental derangement?'

'I don't see why he should. A lot of people are awkward. That doesn't mean they're mad. Ever been to buy a stamp and the clerk just ignores you? Doesn't say "I'm so sorry, I've got to do something else before I can serve you," but just takes no notice of you whatever. That's awkward, if anything is, but the people who do it aren't mad.'

'But why did you make such difficulties about returning the machine? Major Buttonstep called, each of his sons called, you actually made an appointment to give it up and then said they'd got the wrong time. You wouldn't answer the door when they came round. What was the reason for all that?'

'I was being awkward.'

'But why?'

'I've told you. I was provoked.'

'Can you blame my client for thinking that, if you hadn't made away with the machine, you were out of your mind?'

'I certainly can, and I hope the judge will. I tell you, lots of people are awkward, I dare say you've been awkward yourself on occasions, we all are sometimes, but you're not entitled to accuse someone of dishonesty or lunacy just because he's awkward.'

'Don't you realise, Mr Trotter, that, if a person is more than usually awkward, people may think he's out of his mind?'

'It depends what he does.'

'Were you more than usually awkward?'

'That's a difficult question. I was more awkward than I usually am.'

'You admit that?'

'Certainly. Usually I'm not awkward at all.'

'But when you *are* awkward, you are not usually as awkward as this?'

'I didn't say that.'

'Well, are you?'

'I couldn't say. What seems awkward to some people doesn't worry other people. Some people won't let you be awkward, if you see what I mean. If the major hadn't kept on asking for his machine back, I shouldn't have had the chance to be awkward to him.'

'At any rate, you admit that you were particularly awkward to my client?'

'I admit I was awkward. I'm not prepared to agree to any adjectives or adverbs or whatever they are. Awkward I intended to be and awkward I was. And that's all there is to it. If the plaintiff had only said to the policeman: "Mr Trotter's being awkward," I would have had no complaint at all against him. I'd have been glad to hear him say it. Because, if he said I was being awkward, it meant that he felt I was being awkward and when I'm being awkward, I like people to feel it.'

'You wanted to annoy my client?'

'Certainly.'

'D'you think you succeeded?'

'I'm quite sure of it. Look at him. He's bursting with rage even at this moment,' said Mr Trotter, pointing to the major sitting in Court. The major's face reddened, but he controlled himself.

'Behave yourself, Mr Trotter,' said the judge. 'You are not to insult people in the Court.'

'I was only being awkward, your Honour.'

'Well, you're not to be awkward within the precincts of this Court, or …'

'Section 29 or section 139 – I forget which,' said Mr Trotter.

'Mr Larpent,' said the judge, 'I don't like to deal with litigants for contempt of court during the progress of a case, lest they should think that my eventual judgment may in some way be affected by their bad behaviour rather than the evidence. That is why I have shown such latitude to your client up till now. But I cannot overlook his conduct any more. I shall fine him £5 – that is under section 139, Mr Trotter,' he added. 'If he misbehaves again, I shall send him to prison. That will be under section 29. Now let us get on.'

'So you intended to make my client angry,' went on Prunella, 'and you think you succeeded?'

'Yes.'

'A pretty poor return for the kindness he'd shown to you?'

'It was ungrateful, yes. If he'd said that to the policeman I shouldn't have minded. Awkward and ungrateful I may have been, but mad or dishonest certainly not.'

'Have you ever known anyone else in the world,' asked Prunella, 'who has treated such kindness with such ingratitude?'

'Well, that's a large question,' said Mr Trotter. 'As a matter of fact, I don't think I've ever known anyone else to lend a motor mower before – a hand one, yes, but not a motor. People are a bit scared of lending them.'

'So my client was particularly good to you?'

'Unusually so.'

'Don't you think that your persistent awkwardness to my client might reasonably have led him to believe that you were not sane? Here is my client, who has done you an unusual favour, and, instead of being punctilious about returning the machine, you deliberately try and goad him to a fury. Looking back on it, don't you think that the

178

average person would think such ingratitude could only be the product of a warped mind?'

'Well, of course, there isn't an average person. We're always talking of him but there isn't such a thing. Everyone, however ordinary, has some peculiarity of mind or body which most people don't have. Your "average" person is just a fiction. He's just a notional being from whom you have deducted every peculiarity. Well, as her friend said to Mrs Gamp, "I don't believe there's no such a person." So, if you want to ask me a question like that, you must name the person. You must ask me if I think Mr Jones, or Mr Smith or Mr Brown would think so-and-so.'

'Thank you for the lecture,' said Prunella. 'Now I'll ask you again. Do you not think that the ordinary man in the street would have thought you were out of your mind if you'd treated him like that?'

'That's the same question again,' said Mr Trotter, 'There isn't an ordinary man in the street. If you looked out of the window you'd see, say, half a dozen people – one of them would suffer from asthma, another would be claustrophobic, another would have indigestion, another ...'

'That will do,' said the judge. 'You are, of course, in a sense perfectly right, Mr Trotter. There is no average man. But you know quite well what Miss Coombe is referring to ... the people whose peculiarities are not pronounced, who are in fact as near to the notional average man as one can have. What effect do you think your behaviour would have had on such a person?'

'He'd have been annoyed.'

'Yes, yes, we all know that,' said the judge, 'but what Miss Coombe is asking you is – would not such a person reasonably have thought you were out of your mind?'

'Not more than anyone else. We're all out of our mind to some extent – everyone, that is, except the average person – who, of course, doesn't exist. I don't see how anyone could have formed an opinion about my mind without much closer investigation. You're not entitled to assume a person is mad just because he's awkward to you on one particular subject. Now the doctors have investigated me and they're quite satisfied I'm as sane as they are. The plaintiff didn't investigate me at all. He said I was mad because he was angry.'

'Now let me ask you something else,' said Prunella. 'How well did you know the plaintiff's son before you asked to borrow his father's mower?'

'Not well at all. I'd met him twice, I think, perhaps three times.'

'Why did you approach him?'

'I didn't. He approached me.'

'What d'you mean?'

'He told me his father had a motor mower and that he thought he'd lend it to me, if I asked for it.'

'So you say that the idea of the loan came from the plaintiff's son, not from you?'

'I wanted a mower but the plaintiff's son suggested his father might lend me one.'

'Forgive me, your Honour, for one moment,' said Prunella, and whispered to Jane. Jane got up and went and spoke to Digby, who was at the back of the Court. Then she came back and whispered again to Prunella.

'I find you're perfectly right, Mr Trotter,' said Prunella.

'Thank you,' said Mr Trotter. 'You'll find everything I've said has been right. Tell me something that isn't.'

'Don't talk like that,' said the judge. 'Yes, Miss Coombe, any further questions?'

Prunella turned to Jane, who shook her head, and then sat down.

The next witness was PC Glossop, who gave evidence of being consulted by the major and of the events which followed, including the telephone conversation both sides of which he could hear quite plainly. The witness stated that the major had said that Mr Trotter had either stolen the machine or was mad.

'How would you describe Major Buttonstep's condition when he said that?' asked Mr Larpent.

'Condition, sir?' queried PC Glossop, who normally associated the word with alcohol.

'Was he calm, or otherwise?'

'He was annoyed, sir.'

'How annoyed?'

'Pretty annoyed, sir.'

'Did you get the impression that he meant what he said, or did you think he was too angry to think what he was saying?'

'Oh, I think he meant it, sir.'

'Thank you,' said Mr Larpent, and sat down.

'And what view did you take, officer, of the defendant's behaviour?' was Prunella's first question.

'I thought it very odd, miss – I mean ma'am – I er ...'

'You should address your remarks to his Honour. You thought it very odd?'

'I did, your Honour.'

'Had you ever known a person to behave as Mr Trotter behaved?'

'Never, your Honour.'

'Did he sound normal?'

'He sounded normal, your Honour, but he didn't behave normal. He gave no reason for not returning the

181

machine. Yet he wouldn't return it, and he wouldn't answer the door.'

'Did you think he was sane, officer?'

'I must say I wondered, your Honour.'

'What about the machine – did you think he might have stolen it?'

'Well – er – your Honour, I didn't think he could have stolen it because it was lent to him. But it was possible he'd made away with it, converted it.'

'Did you think he'd converted it?'

'I can't say that I did, Miss – I mean, your Honour.'

'Why not?'

'Because he admitted he'd had it. He was living in the house. He couldn't help but be found out if he had sold it or anything.'

'Then why did you think he was behaving as he did?'

'I couldn't think for the life of me,' said PC Glossop.

Prunella sat down and Mr Larpent got up.

'Unless, perhaps, officer,' he said, 'he was trying to be awkward? That would have explained it, wouldn't it?'

Jane nudged Prunella, who stood up.

'Those are very leading questions,' she said. 'My learned friend oughtn't to put the words into the witness' mouth.'

'I apologise,' said Mr Larpent. 'My learned friend is perfectly right. Well, officer, what is the answer to the question?'

'It could have been that, sir.'

'Thank you, officer,' said Mr Larpent, and PC Glossop left the witness box.

'That is the defendant's case, your Honour,' said Mr Larpent, and sat down.

CHAPTER FOURTEEN

Major Buttonstep's Case

'I'll call the plaintiff straight away,' said Prunella, and the major went into the box and took the oath. Then, in reply to Prunella, he described how he came to lend the mowing machine and the efforts he made to get it back. Finally Prunella asked him: 'When you said that the defendant had either stolen the machine or was mad, what did you believe?'

'I believed what I said to be true. I still believe it.'

Prunella sat down. Mr Larpent got up.

'You still believe it to be true, do you?' he asked.

'Certainly.'

'So you believe he's stolen your machine?'

'Well, I haven't had it back, have I? We've only his word that he's still got it. If he's sane, I don't believe he's still got it. If he's still got it, I think he's mad.'

'Well, it can easily be tested – if his Honour agrees. We can all go down to the house and see if it's there. My client is quite prepared to agree to that.'

'If we do that, perhaps I can be allowed to take it away – if it's there.'

'That's another matter,' said Mr Larpent.

'Why shouldn't he take it away,' asked the judge, 'if it's there. Your client has admitted that his excuses for not giving up the machine were made in order to be awkward. So, subject to anything you may say, it seems to me that the plaintiff's case is amply proved. Your client is not entitled to hold on to the machine in case he gets any damages for slander. I quite agree that it might be a good thing if the solicitors on each side went down during the luncheon adjournment to see if the machine is there. If it is, it ought to be handed over there and then if the plaintiff can make arrangements to take it away.'

'With the greatest possible respect,' said Mr Larpent, 'I am entitled to address your Honour on the matter first.'

'All right, Mr Larpent. Address me now, please.'

'What, your Honour, in the middle of cross-examining the plaintiff?'

'Are there any questions you wish to ask him relating to the claim, or will your cross-examination relate only to the defendant's claim for slander?'

'In view of my client's frankness my questions will relate only to the slander.'

'Very well, then, Mr Larpent, kindly say whatever you want about the claim now.'

'Well your Honour, with the greatest possible respect – and I am sure your Honour knows me well enough to appreciate that I intend no discourtesy to your Honour – with the greatest possible respect, I must decline your Honour's invitation.'

'Then I take it you have no grounds to urge why an order for the immediate return of the machine should not be made?'

'I didn't say that, your Honour. I said I was not prepared to make my submissions at this stage.'

'Well, Mr Larpent, I will give you the opportunity of saying anything you wish about the claim, and, unless you do, I propose to deliver judgment upon it.'

'But – but …' Mr Larpent almost stammered in his expostulation, 'but – you can't do that in the middle of the plaintiff's cross-examination.'

'Can't I?' said the judge. 'You're just going to hear me.'

'But, your Honour, it puts me in a very great difficulty.'

'I can't see why, Mr Larpent, but, if it does, I'm quite sure you are capable of coping with it.'

'That is very good of your Honour, but, with the greatest possible respect …'

'Never mind about the respect, Mr Larpent. Kindly make up your mind whether you are going to address me.'

'Very well, then, your Honour,' said Mr Larpent, 'I will reserve my client's rights and say nothing. But I ask your Honour to make a note of my most respectful protest.'

'I will do so, Mr Larpent.'

The judge wrote for about half a minute.

'That will be sufficient for you in the Court of Appeal, or the Divisional Court or wherever you like to go.'

Major Buttonstep, who had up till now formed a high opinion of Judge Smoothe, almost howled in despair. He knew it. It was going to be the poacher all over again. Court of Appeal or Divisional Court! Why had he ever started the thing! He'd be in the House of Lords before he finished. This time he simply hadn't got the money with which to pay the costs. He tiptoed up to Jane and asked her to come outside the Court. They went out.

'You must stop him,' he said. 'Believe me, I know the form. I don't care whether he's right or wrong, whether I get my mowing machine back or not, but I'm not going to the House of Lords or anywhere else. I'd rather lose the case. Tell your sister to stop him.'

Jane went hurriedly back into Court, to find the judge poised to give judgment and actually clearing his throat for the purpose.

'Stop him, Prunella,' she said. 'Say you don't want judgment yet.'

'In this case,' began the judge – when Prunella got up. She felt extremely nervous. It was a terrible thing to interrupt a judge in the middle of his judgment. She had never seen it done before. She was glad it was Judge Smoothe and not some of the other judges she knew. As she stood there anxiously, her frightened mind could visualise what would follow: 'Sit down, Miss Coombe,' he would say.

Normally she would obey the command, but there was much more in this case than just winning it. She had got to do what Major Buttonstep wanted. That was all that mattered. If it had been anybody else's case she would have told her client not to be silly. After all, the judge was going to give judgment in his favour. It was true that it was a rather unorthodox way of doing so. But, as there was now clearly no defence to the claim, how could the defendant be prejudiced?

'Well, what is it?' asked the judge, not too amiably. He was aware that the procedure he was following was, to say the least of it, unusual. But he could see no harm in it, and in such circumstances, he did not mind breaking the rules. He was quite prepared for Mr Trotter to take the case to a higher Court. In fact he would be quite interested to see what the Divisional Court or Court of Appeal would say about it.

'I do apologise for interrupting, your Honour,' said Prunella, 'but my client would rather wait until the end of the case for the return of his mower.'

For one moment Judge Smoothe almost lost his head.

'So you think I'm wrong too, do you?' he said, and immediately regretted it. It was petty and undignified, and he could not remember having done such a thing before.

Perhaps everyone was being affected by Mr Trotter's strange behaviour.

'No, indeed, your Honour,' said Prunella. 'I'm quite sure your Honour is right.'

'Then what are you worrying about?'

'My client doesn't want the case to go to a higher court, even though he wins there. He and his family have unfortunately had a great deal of experience in litigation. I do hope your Honour will forgive my intervening.'

'Very well,' said the judge, 'as neither of you want me to give judgment at this stage, I won't do so. But, in view of the fact that I was proposing to take a course to which you objected, Mr Larpent, would you like the whole case to be reheard before another judge?'

'Indeed, not as far as I am concerned,' said Mr Larpent. 'But perhaps I had better ask my client. In saying that, I do assure your Honour that I do not intend the least disrespect to your Honour, and that I personally hope that your Honour will continue with the case. I know that your Honour will not be unfairly prejudiced by anything that has happened. It is not as if there were a jury and …'

'Do consult your client, please, Mr Larpent,' interrupted the judge. 'I am quite sure that you are incapable of the least disrespect to the court.'

'Your Honour is very kind and I am most obliged.'

'Do consult your client,' urged the judge, who knew that Mr Larpent, unless seriously discouraged, was quite capable of demonstrating his greatest possible respect and repeating interminably how exceedingly much obliged he was.

'If your Honour pleases,' said Mr Larpent, 'I will do so immediately. I am most grateful to your Honour for the opportunity. If I may say so …'

'No,' said the judge, 'you may not. Consult your client, please.'

'At once, your Honour,' said Mr Larpent. 'If your Honour will allow me to take him outside the Court so that I can explain to him the full implications of …'

'I will allow anything if you will consult your client,' said the judge.

'It's very good of your Honour. Then, with your Honour's permission, I will …'

'You have it – you have it, Mr Larpent. Kindly take your client outside the Court and explain matters to him, and don't let's waste any more time.'

At last Mr Larpent was persuaded to stop talking, and everyone waited while he went out of the Court with Mr Trotter and Mr Dealtry.

Outside the Court Mr Trotter said: 'What's all this in aid of?'

'It's my duty to explain to you as your counsel,' said Mr Larpent, 'exactly what the situation is.'

'That's what I asked,' said Mr Trotter, who had become about as irritated with Mr Larpent's long-windedness as the judge. Mr Larpent then explained that the judge had offered Mr Trotter a new trial before a different judge.

'Why?' asked Mr Trotter. 'One's enough, isn't it?'

'The reason is because he had proposed to do something irregular. Now he's not going to do it, he doesn't want you to appeal if you lose the case because of what he was going to do. You see, by offering you a new trial, he prevents your complaining of his behaviour if you decide to go on with the case before him.'

'Wily old devil,' said Mr Trotter. 'Where did he learn that trick?'

'I don't think you should speak of the learned judge like that,' said Mr Larpent, who was respectful to judges, not only in Court but to his clients and even in his dreams.

'Why not?' asked Mr Trotter. 'You won't tell him, will you?'

'Of course not,' said Mr Larpent, and started to launch into an explanation of the relationship between a barrister and his client. But Mr Trotter became bored with this.

'OK,' he said, 'we'll go on.'

'Are you quite sure?' asked Mr Larpent. 'I don't want there to be any misunderstanding.'

'I said OK,' said Mr Trotter, 'because I meant OK.'

'Very well,' said Mr Larpent. 'I'll inform the judge.'

They went back into Court.

'My client will be delighted if your Honour will be good enough to go on with the case,' said Mr Larpent.

'I didn't say "delighted,"' said Mr Trotter in a whisper to Mr Dealtry. 'I only said "OK".'

'That's all right, Mr Trotter,' whispered Mr Dealtry, 'that's just the legal way of putting it.'

'I am most grateful to your Honour for giving me the opportunity of conferring with my client, and so is he.'

'Very well,' said the judge. 'Now let's get on. Where were we?'

'I was cross-examining the plaintiff about his belief. Will you go back into the box, please, Major Buttonstep?'

The major returned to the box.

'Now suppose,' went on Mr Larpent, 'the machine is at Mr Trotter's house, do you say on your oath that you think he is a lunatic?'

'Certainly I do. Why should a sane man cause all this bother and expense?'

'You've heard his explanation – that he wanted to be awkward to you. Don't you believe it?'

189

'I think that anyone who wanted to be as awkward as Mr Trotter was to me must be out of his mind.'

'Do you still say that, although doctors have examined him and found him to be sane?'

'In that case I think the doctors want examining.'

'That is your answer, is it?' asked Mr Larpent. 'That the doctors are insane?'

'Well, I don't see how any sane man who was told how the defendant had behaved could think Mr Trotter was sane.'

'But your solicitor and counsel have admitted that Mr Trotter is sane.'

'Perhaps he's recovered, though he doesn't give much sign of it.'

'No, that won't do, Major Buttonstep. Your advisers have admitted that the defendant was at all material times sane.'

'I don't know what that means.'

'It means that they admit he was sane while you were talking to Constable Glossop.'

'Well, I repeat that, if he was sane then, he's made away with the machine.'

'But your advisers admit that the defendant was sane while you were talking to Constable Glossop.'

'They can admit what they like, I'm telling you what I believe.'

'But you can't,' said Mr Larpent.

'Well, I have,' said the major.

'And why shouldn't he?' asked the judge. 'It is admitted on behalf of the plaintiff that Mr Trotter is in fact neither dishonest nor insane. But that doesn't mean that the plaintiff doesn't and didn't *believe* him to be one or the other. The real question is whether he did honestly have that belief when he spoke in the presence of the policeman.'

'If your Honour pleases,' said Mr Larpent. 'Now, Major Buttonstep, did you not appreciate when you were speaking in front of Constable Glossop that it was a very serious thing to say a man has stolen your machine?'

'Less serious than stealing it. How would you like it if a complete stranger borrowed something from you and then treated you as Mr Trotter treated me?'

'You mustn't ask me questions,' said Mr Larpent.

'That's quite true,' said the judge, 'but I'd have been interested to hear the answer. I think we'll adjourn for lunch now, and during the adjournment you can ascertain if the machine is still on the defendant's premises.'

The Court rose and Major Buttonstep took his two legal advisers and his two sons to lunch at the Buttonstep Arms.

'How's it going, major?' asked Archie.

'Sh,' said the major, 'he's just behind me.'

And a moment later Mr Trotter walked in with Mr Dealtry and occupied a table next to the major's. The conversation on both sides was accordingly very much restricted. For the most part they discussed in loud, rather self-conscious voices, all manner of subjects unconnected with the law, mowing machines or slander. At one stage it looked as though Mr Trotter was deliberately baiting the major for, as soon as one of the major's party started a new topic, Mr Trotter began to talk to Mr Dealtry on the same subject. Later on he actually tried to get the two parties engaged in conversation with each other. The major had asked Archie, who was standing by the sideboard in the dining-room, what was likely to win the St Leger.

'Yes,' Mr Trotter joined in, 'what's your view?' And then, before Archie could answer, he added, addressing his question to the major: 'You much of a punter?'

The major ignored the question and turned towards Archie.

'I can give you something hot for the 3.30 tomorrow, major,' said Mr Trotter.

The major had excellent manners and although he had felt justified in the circumstances in ignoring the first question, he could not go on pretending that Mr Trotter was not in the room.

'No, thank you,' he said.

'Go on,' said Mr Trotter. 'Be a sport. I don't want anything out of it. Just say "yes" and the horse is yours.'

'No, thank you,' repeated the major.

'What about you, landlord?' asked Mr Trotter.

'What's the horse?' asked Archie.

'Screwey,' said Mr Trotter.

'Hasn't a chance,' said Archie, 'not with that weight.'

'They've got a seven-pound apprentice on him.'

'Too difficult for a boy to hold.'

'It's young Mansfield. He's ridden him before.'

'Mansfield, is it?' said Archie. 'How d'you know?'

'There's a lot I know,' said Mr Trotter, 'but I'm not always as forthcoming about it. But I feel in a good mood today. I've got a case on at the County Court. P'raps you've heard of it. Oh – sorry, major, I forgot you were here.'

After lunch the parties made a hurried visit to Mr Trotter's house where the mowing machine was duly inspected. The major could not make up his mind whether he was glad to see it or not. He was, however, glad to notice that no blades appeared to be broken.

After the inspection they all went back to the Court and the case was resumed.

'You now have seen,' said Mr Larpent, continuing his cross-examination of the major, 'that the defendant has not made away with the mower.'

'He's got it now,' said the major, 'but how am I to know that he hasn't bought it back for the purposes of the case?'

'Are you suggesting that my client in fact converted the machine?'

'I've no idea what you mean by that,' said the major, 'but I'm suggesting nothing. I'm telling you that, in my belief, your client is either dishonest or insane.'

'You've said that before,' said Mr Larpent.

'And I'll say it again,' said the major, 'whenever you ask me the same question.'

CHAPTER FIFTEEN

Judgment

For a further two hours Mr Larpent continued to cross-examine the major and at the end of that time the judge adjourned for the day. That night Prunella and Jane discussed together in detail what Prunella should say in her final speech. They went over the whole ground together and worked on the case as if their lives were at stake. Every single point which could be made against Mr Trotter was duly noted by Prunella. When they'd extracted everything they could think of from the material at their disposal, they went to their father, who suggested a few further points. Finally, they went to bed and Prunella had strange dreams of Mr Trotter chasing the judge round the Court while the major sat in the judge's seat with Jane on his lap.

The evidence was concluded the next morning and Prunella got up to fire off the considerable amount of ammunition which she and Jane had collected the night before. She was nervous but had the confidence which full preparation gives to an advocate. There, on the table before her, were notes of all the points which she proposed to make. She need not worry about forgetting one for, before concluding her speech, she could look through her notes to see if she had missed anything. It is only the few people with brains like Archie Randall's who do not require a carefully prepared note. It was to be the most important speech she had ever made – and perhaps ever would make – in her life. If the major lost his case, there could be no question of his being a happy consenting party to having Jane and Prunella as daughters-in-law. Even if he won it, it was by no means certain that they would be acceptable in that capacity. But at least there was a chance, if he won. There was none, if he didn't. Digby and John and Jane waited anxiously for Prunella to begin, Jane being ready to prompt her should she ever need it. The nerves of all four of them were like those of the competitors in a top-class sprint race, when the starter has to be particularly good if a false start is to be avoided.

The most common fault among starters is to hold the runners too long. And certainly, if Judge Smoothe had started a hundred yards' race as he started the final round of *Buttonstep v Trotter*, he would have come in for a good deal of legitimate criticism. First of all he adjusted the rug on his knees, then he took off his spectacles, cleaned them and put them on again, turned over a few pages in his notebook, called the usher and whispered to him, spoke to his clerk, asked for a window to be opened – ('No, not that one – the one over there') – demanded a new pencil – ('I do like a sharp point, Mr Crawley') – picked up some of the papers in front of him, put them down again, blew his nose, first removing his spectacles, dropped them on the ground, made a few ineffective attempts to pick them up himself, dislodging his rug in the process, called for the usher to pick up the spectacles and replace the rug, shifted himself in his chair and eventually sat back in it with an air of finality.

'Yes, Miss Coombe?' he said, but, before Prunella could get started, he had added, 'Just one moment, please,' and picked up some papers and started looking at them.

Certainly the spectators at the White City would have had something to say of a starter who went through motions equivalent to those of Judge Smoothe before unleashing the highly-strung, tense competitors.

Prunella waited patiently for the gun. And finally it came, but not before the judge had repeated nearly all of his previous activities and had further discussions with the usher and his clerk and lost his rug and his spectacles again in the process. And, when he did fire it, it was something of a bathos. As Prunella stood there ready to remind the judge of the iniquities of Mr Trotter, and of the generosity and patience of the major, the judge simply shook his head at her and said: 'I need not trouble you, Miss Coombe.'

Although Prunella knew from this that the judge intended to decide in her favour, unless anything which Mr Larpent said changed his mind (in which case he would give her a chance of trying to change it back again), she felt very much like a pricked balloon as she sat down. Jane hurried to tell the major what had happened, lest he should imagine that further injustices were being perpetrated on the Buttonstep family.

Mr Larpent then got up and began: 'It would be idle to pretend,' he said, 'that I do not realise, from the indication your Honour has given by not calling on my learned friend, that the task before me is a heavy one. But, if I may say so with respect, I know your Honour will keep an open mind until I have finally said everything there is to be said on my client's behalf. The task of counsel addressing a learned judge who has intimated that he is against him on presumably every point is not an easy one, but,

a very difficult question of fact on which he considers the opinion of a body of laymen preferable to that of a single lawyer. I say it because I should like the defendant to have heard the opinion of a body of laymen – I won't say men like himself, but of ordinary men and women – about this case. I have myself no doubt whatever about the matter and I cannot conceive that any jury would have to come to a view in any way different from my own. In spite of Mr Larpent's eloquent submissions, I have come to the clear conclusion that the plaintiff's claim in this matter should not have been resisted and that the defendant's counter claim should never have been made. Apart from his perhaps rather ill-advised, though quite understandable, attempt to regain his own property, the plaintiff's conduct in all the matters relating to this case has been exactly what one would expect of a decent, fair minded, generous Englishman. The defendant's behaviour, on the other hand, has, in my view – and I do not intend to mince my words on this matter – although it is admitted that he is in fact sane – his conduct has been that of a lunatic. Having regard to the admissions made on the plaintiff's behalf and to the evidence of the defendant himself, I am prepared to accept – indeed, I must accept that the defendant is quite sane, and his conduct, therefore, was in fact due to a peculiarly unpleasant quality in his character which prompted him to repay Major Buttonstep's exceptional kindness to a stranger by deliberate acts of base ingratitude. I accept that, in behaving as he did, Mr Trotter was – to use his own words – being awkward. But no normal person could expect another normal person to behave with such awkwardness. I haven't the least doubt that any ordinary person placed in Major Buttonstep's position would certainly have thought and would probably have said: "This man is either a thief or a lunatic." And now, if you please, Mr Trotter, who has caused all this trouble by his deliberate awkwardness, has the temerity to come to this Court and ask for damages because Major Buttonstep said what most people would have said. The facts have only to be stated to show how ludicrous the defendant's claim is. If, indeed, the occasion were not privileged, I should consider a farthing damages grossly excessive, and, as the farthing has now been abolished, I suppose I should have had to award a halfpenny which would have been twice as much. However, I am glad to be able to come to the conclusion that what the plaintiff said was said on an occasion which was in fact privileged. The plaintiff was speaking only in the presence of the local police constable and he was trying to regain possession of his own property. He plainly had a right to say anything relevant to the repossession of that property in the truth of which he honestly believed. Now, it's quite true – and I don't blame the plaintiff for this – that, when he spoke the words complained of, he was angry. Anyone but a saint would have been angry. But I am equally satisfied that, though angry, the plaintiff honestly believed that what he said was true. He has been cross-examined before me at very considerable length, and the longer the cross-examination went on the plainer it appeared to me that the plaintiff was a witness of truth who honestly believed, and still honestly believes in, the accuracy of what he said about the defendant. I have so far been discussing the counterclaim. I did so deliberately because at least there was something to discuss in it. Undoubtedly it is defamatory to say of a man that he is either mad or dishonest, and, once it is admitted that he is neither, the only defence to such a claim for slander is privilege. For the reasons I have stated, that defence succeeds and the counterclaim accordingly fails. As far as the claim is concerned, there is nothing to discuss at all. There is no defence whatever to the plaintiff's claim and the defendant has behaved disgracefully in not returning the plaintiff's property to him. I shall accordingly order the defendant to deliver up the machine to the plaintiff immediately and in addition, I shall award £30 damages for the detention. I should make it plain that £15 of that sum is for the inconvenience suffered by the plaintiff in being without his machine, and the balance is punitive damages having regard to the circumstances in which the defendant deliberately withheld the machine from the plaintiff. Those damages are to be paid forthwith and the defendant must also bear the whole of the costs of claim and counterclaim on the highest County Scale – Scale 4.'

Mr Larpent then got up.

'Would your Honour grant a stay of execution pending an appeal?' he asked.

'Certainly not,' said the judge. 'What is there to appeal about?'

'The punitive damages for one thing, your Honour.'

'Your client is lucky I didn't award £400 against him. I shall grant no stay of any kind. You must go to the Court of Appeal if you want one.'

'But, your Honour, as your Honour has ordered the immediate return of the machine, there won't be time to get to the Court of Appeal to ask for a stay of execution there.'

'And a good thing, too,' said the judge. 'And thank you for reminding me. I shall authorise the Court to give priority to the issue of the warrant for delivery of this machine. Miss Coombe, if your client chooses to go into the office and issue the warrant, I will say that a bailiff should go and execute it at once.'

'I am very much obliged to your Honour,' said Prunella. While Jane was going into the County Court office to issue the warrant, Mr Larpent and Mr Dealtry were conferring with their client. Within five minutes they were running out of the Court towards Mr Dealtry's car. Major Buttonstep saw them and reported the matter to Jane. The effect was immediate.

'Whose is the fastest car?' she asked.

Digby volunteered that his would do 120 mph on the M1.

'Come on, quick,' said Jane, and within a few minutes she and Prunella and the major and his two sons were speeding after the defendant. Jane explained as they went along: 'I bet they're going to the Court of Appeal to try to get a stay of execution before the bailiff has time to call. The Court rises at 4.15 – so they should get there in time.'

'We'll catch them in this,' said Digby. 'Shall we ram them?'

'Oh, no,' said Jane, 'I should be struck off the Rolls and Prunella would be disbarred.'

'Do you mean to say?' said the major, 'that if we hadn't seen what they were at, the Appeal Court might have stopped the judge's order going through?'

'It might,' said Jane, 'though only for a day or two. The most they'd have done would have been to grant what we call a stay for a few days, and then we'd have been able to give the Court our version of the matter. But, if we can get there now, with luck we shall stop them granting a stay at all, if Prunella does her stuff. Come on, Digby, where's that 120 you were speaking of?'

'This isn't the M1, Jane,' said Digby. 'We certainly would never get to Court if I tried it here.'

Copplestone was not far from London but there was plenty of traffic and it was twenty minutes to four when

Prunella rushed into the robing room, put on her robes and dashed up the stairs to the Court of Appeal, where Jane and the major and the two brothers were anxiously waiting for her.

'Quick,' said Jane, 'they've just finished an appeal, and Larpent's getting up.'

As Prunella went in through the swing doors, Mr Larpent was saying: 'My Lords, might I make to your Lordships an urgent *ex parte* application?'

'What is it?' said the presiding judge, Lord Justice Crewe.

'It is for a stay of execution for a few days until I can serve notice of appeal and of an application for a stay until the appeal can be heard.'

'What was the nature of the action?'

Mr Larpent told the Court what the action was about and what the judge had ordered.

'My Lords,' he went on, 'if I may respectfully say so, it can do no harm if the warrant is stayed for a few days until the application can be fully heard. The learned judge, however, not only refused a stay but actually said that he would accelerate execution of the warrant. If I may say so, with the greatest possible respect to the learned judge, and without intending the slightest impertinence, I have never heard a learned judge do that before.'

'Well, I've done it, Mr Larpent,' said Lord Justice Crewe. 'Of course, it should only be done in a proper case, and presumably the learned judge thought this was one.'

'I must confess,' said Lord Justice Blake, 'that I don't see what harm it can do for the defendant to keep the machine for a couple of days until you can serve notice. The grass can't grow much in that time.'

'But, my Lords,' broke in Prunella, prompted by Jane.

'What are you doing here, Miss Coombe?' asked Lord Justice Crewe. He would not normally have known her name, but, as the daughter of Mr Justice Coombe, he had seen her at a number of legal gatherings. 'Have you come up from Copplestone too?' added the Lord Justice.

'Yes my Lord,' said Prunella.

'I hope you didn't exceed the speed limit,' said another member of the Court.

'I wasn't driving myself,' said Prunella, 'and I would rather not make any statement on the subject.'

'Why should we hear you?' said Lord Justice Blake. 'Mr Larpent only wants a stay for a couple of days. That can't hurt you, surely?'

'The learned judge took a very strong view about the case,' said Prunella.

'So I gather,' said Lord Justice Blake, 'but, with great respect to him, that doesn't necessarily mean that he was right. I once took a strong view of a case, and all the judges in the Court of Appeal said I was wrong. I still think *they* were, but they reversed my judgment all the same.'

'My Lords,' said Prunella, 'this is admittedly the plaintiff's mowing machine. In the witness box the defendant agreed that he had deliberately refused to return it to the plaintiff in order to be, as he himself said, awkward. My Lords, why shouldn't the plaintiff have the machine back at once?'

'Is what Miss Coombe says correct?' Lord Justice Crewe asked Mr Larpent.

'My Lords,' said Mr Larpent, 'I have to agree that it is, but I should like to urge upon your Lordships …'

'Well, if it's correct, why on earth shouldn't the mower be returned at once? Forgive me for using the word "earth" in this connection,' said Lord Justice Crewe.

'Well, my Lords,' began Mr Larpent.

'I'm not surprised the learned judge took a strong view about the case,' said Lord Justice Blake.

'But, my Lords,' protested Mr Larpent, 'with the greatest possible respect …'

'On what you've admitted,' said Lord Justice Crewe, 'the learned judge seems to have been perfectly right.'

'With the greatest possible respect, my Lords …'

'Have you issued your notice of appeal yet?' asked Lord Justice Crewe.

'We haven't had time,' said Mr Larpent.

'Then I don't see why we should hear you any more,' said the Lord Justice. 'If there were some grave injury threatened to your client it might be another matter. Injustice usually takes precedence over technicalities. But, as far as I can see, the only injustice here is to the plaintiff, whose mowing machine your client appears to have kept merely in order to annoy him. I'm not surprised the learned judge was indignant.'

'Oh, my Lord, I only said he took a strong view.'

'Well, you can say that I'm indignant,' said Lord Justice Crewe. 'The defendant appears to have behaved outrageously. We will not hear you any more, Mr Larpent.'

'But, my Lords …'

'I ask that the application be dismissed with costs,' said Prunella.

'I submit your Lordships have no power to order costs,' said Mr Larpent. 'My learned friend oughtn't to be here at all.'

'I'll bet he wishes she hadn't been,' whispered the major to Jane. He was beginning to feel rather like an unsuccessful punter who, having been taken unwillingly to a racecourse, had backed the first two winners. It was a new and pleasant experience.

'If we hadn't been here,' said Prunella, 'your Lordships might have granted the application.'

'That's certainly a point,' said Lord Justice Blake. 'It would seem very hard on the plaintiff that his advisers should race all the way from Copplestone to stop an order being made and that he should have to pay the costs of their doing so.'

'But if your Lordships have no power,' began Mr Larpent but he got no further.

'Haven't we an overriding discretion about costs?' put in Lord Justice Crewe. 'It's true that this was an *ex parte* application. But the plaintiff's counsel was here and we did listen to her. And, furthermore, what she said to us made a difference. I think the plaintiff ought to have his costs, and, if that isn't the law, it ought to be.'

The three judges discussed the matter in whispers for a short time and then Lord Justice Crewe announced their decision.

'The plaintiff is to have his costs of coming here.'

'And I hope it doesn't rain before the machine is returned,' said Lord Justice Blake.

CHAPTER SIXTEEN

Warrant of Delivery

While the proceedings were going on in the Court of Appeal a bailiff from Copplestone County Court was unsuccessfully trying to execute the warrant of delivery. He attended at Mr Trotter's house but could obtain no answer. He waited for half an hour and finally returned to Copplestone. The chief clerk advised him to go back first thing in the morning. It was in fact just as well for the bailiff that Mr Trotter had been out, for it would have been impossible for him to remove the machine. He had gone to Mr Trotter's house on a motorcycle and, while he could push the mowing machine or the cycle, he certainly could not have pushed both at the same time.

The next morning he borrowed the registrar's stationwagon and on this occasion he was more successful. Mr Trotter actually opened the door and invited him in.

'It's very good of you to come,' he said. 'What about a glass of beer?'

'That's very good of you, sir,' said the bailiff. Mr Trotter filled two glasses and gave one to the bailiff.

'Your very good health,' he said.

'My best respects, sir,' said the bailiff.

From what he had been told by the chief clerk at the County Court he had not expected this treatment. Then suddenly it occurred to him that the idea was to make him drunk. Well, he was proof against that. It would take a good deal more than half a pint of beer to achieve that object. But perhaps it was drugged. He took his next drink more sparingly. It tasted all right. But did he detect a faint bitterness? He did. But in fact it was no more than is usual in beer.

'Perhaps I could collect the machine and finish this afterwards, sir,' he said.

'Certainly,' said Mr Trotter. 'Duty first. Let me help you.'

He led the bailiff to a shed in the back garden, opened it and pulled out the machine.

'Here we are,' he said. 'All ship-shape. I can't think what all the fuss was about. However, it's saved me a lot of trouble your coming over for it. Otherwise I'd have had to lug it over myself. You must get some odd cases in your job.'

'We do sometimes,' said the bailiff, 'but it's a great pleasure to have to deal with a gentleman like yourself.'

'Only too pleased to be of help.'

'I expect it was all the result of a misunderstanding, sir?'

'The whole thing was cock-eyed, if you ask me,' said Mr Trotter. 'But one lives and learns. You take my advice: never borrow a mowing machine. I've never borrowed one before and it won't happen again. It'll be the most expensive loan I've ever had from anyone. What d'you think the costs will be?'

'Well, I wouldn't rightly know, sir,' said the bailiff. 'That isn't exactly my department. But they shouldn't be more than £100.'

'£100!' said Mr Trotter. '£100 to have to listen to all that nonsense? What'll it cost Major Buttonstep?'

'I meant those would be his costs, sir, which you've been ordered to pay.'

'D'you mean to say I've got to pay my own costs as well?'

'I'm afraid so, sir.'

'They'll be more than £100, I suppose?'

'They might be, sir.'

'Well, it's really too bad. £200 to borrow a mowing machine. I could have bought a couple for less.'

'It's most unfortunate, sir,' said the bailiff. Between them they lifted the mower into the registrar's wagon and returned to finish their beer.

'They did say that you were going to appeal, sir,' said the bailiff. 'Would that be right?'

'What would you advise?' asked Mr Trotter. 'Is it a good thing to appeal?'

'Well, sir, if you lose, it costs you twice as much.'

'D'you think I'd lose?'

'Well, sir, I wouldn't rightly know, but they do say that Judge Smoothe doesn't often make a mistake.'

'Would you give him a message for me?' asked Mr Trotter.

'I'm afraid I couldn't do that, sir.'

'It would be quite a short one.'

'If you wrote a letter to the registrar I could deliver it for you, sir.'

'A letter? It wouldn't be a letter. Just a couple of words or so.'

'I couldn't do that, sir.'

'Perhaps I could telephone.'

'Well, of course, sir, that's up to you. But if I were you, sir, I'd forget the whole thing. That's best and cheapest in the long run.'

'Good gracious,' said Mr Trotter, 'I'd never thought of that. It's quite an idea. Have the other half.'

'Well, I don't mind if I do, sir.'

In consequence of this interview the opinion held at Copplestone County Court as a result of the bailiff's report was that Mr Trotter was crackers but a gentleman.

CHAPTER SEVENTEEN

Daughters in Law

Three months later Major Buttonstep gave a small dinner party and the judge and his wife attended. It was to celebrate the official engagements of Digby and John with Prunella and Jane. The judge's diagnosis of the major's hatred of lawyers appeared to have been accurate. Litigation was in the Buttonstep blood and it was only years of costly and unsuccessful litigation which had given the major his view on the subject. But now four judges had each expressed himself in strong language in favour of the major and had severely criticised his opponent. And not only that, but Mr Trotter, whatever else might be said against him, had paid the major's costs in full.

Rather sheepishly at first, the major had had to admit that, when the law was his only weapon, it had not failed him. It was true that he had had to go to the Court of Appeal but only for a very short time and it had cost him nothing. Perhaps the law wasn't such a bad fellow after all. Not long after the defeat of Mr Trotter, he had actually started to ask the girls about their cases, and within quite a short time after that, he freely assented to the two marriages.

At the celebration dinner the case was, of course, discussed.

'He must have been a lunatic after all,' said the judge.

'You must forgive my disagreeing,' said the major. 'As a matter of fact, I've had some experience of lunatics. I used to visit the hospital at Speckley regularly. Of course, at first I thought he was mad, if he hadn't stolen the machine. But in the end, having observed him in Court for a considerable time, I was satisfied that he was perfectly sane. Indeed, I believed the man. He was one of those people who cannot bear to be crossed and so, in his own words, he set out to be awkward. You may, of course, say that so much awkwardness can amount to insanity, but, except to that extent, in my view, he was no lunatic.'

'Well, major,' said the judge, 'if you say that with your experience, I expect you're right. And that means I must have been wrong. Because I warned the girls that there was something behind the case which none of us knew and I warned them to look out for it. Well, it only shows that odd things do happen and that you mustn't be too sure that you haven't heard the whole truth just because what you hear *seems* incomplete. I must confess that until now I felt sure I was right. But I suppose I can't have been.'

But the judge *was*, in fact, right. There *was* something in the case which never came to light. Digby and John drove the girls home at the end of the dinner party. On the way Prunella said: 'You know, we really owe all this to Mr Trotter. We should never have brought your father round but for him.'

'Yes,' said Jane. 'That's true. And he's the only one left out of the celebrations. All he's had to do is to pay the costs, your father's and his own as well. And now he's had to leave the neighbourhood. At least I suppose he felt he had to. I'm so grateful to him. I almost feel sorry for him.'

'So do I,' said Prunella.

'Oh, I expect he's managed all right,' said Digby.

And, indeed, Mr Trotter – for an out-of-work author and actor – had managed very well indeed. Entirely financed by Digby and John he had had six months' free living at Buttonstep, a weekly salary and, of course, all his legal costs paid. When Digby first discovered him his name was Walker and he reverted to that name when he left the Buttonstep neighbourhood.

Mr Justice Coombe had put the idea into Digby's head when he said that a one-time racing man will start betting again if he wins a couple of bets. So Digby and John had looked for a likely candidate to force their father into litigation and then to let him have a nice comfortable victory. From Mr Walker's point of view it was an admirable suggestion. He committed no offence, what he said in the witness box was true, he was kept in comfort for six months, and he earned much more than he would have been likely to earn at either of his professions. In case his odd behaviour might ever prejudice him in the future he had grown a beard for the part, and it was in the highest degree unlikely that, even supposing he did subsequently meet someone from Buttonstep, the clean-shaven and very ordinary Mr Walker would be associated with the bearded and awkward Mr Trotter. He left Buttonstep in a very happy frame of mind. It was the longest run he had ever known, and no words of his had ever had such a wide circulation.

Digby would have liked to thank the judge for giving him the idea, but both he and his brother thought that, on the whole, this was a secret to be kept even from their wives, at any rate for a good many years.

Not long after the double wedding the major came into Jane's office in a state of some excitement and asked to see her.

'A chap's just run into my front gate and done no end of damage,' he told her.

'I'm terribly sorry,' said Jane, 'but I suppose you're insured?'

'Insured be blowed,' said the major. 'I'm going to sue the fellow.'

HENRY CECIL

ACCORDING TO THE EVIDENCE

Alec Morland is on trial for murder. He has tried to remedy the ineffectiveness of the law by taking matters into his own hands. Unfortunately for him, his alleged crime was not committed in immediate defence of others or of himself. In this fascinating murder trial you will not find out until the very end just how the law will interpret his actions. Will his defence be accepted or does a different fate await him?

THE ASKING PRICE

Ronald Holbrook is a fifty-seven-year-old bachelor who has lived in the same house for twenty years. Jane Doughty, the daughter of his next-door neighbours, is seventeen. She suddenly decides she is in love with Ronald and wants to marry him. Everyone is amused at first but then events take a disturbingly sinister turn and Ronald finds himself enmeshed in a potentially tragic situation.

'The secret of Mr Cecil's success lies in continuing to do superbly what everyone now knows he can do well.'
The Sunday Times

HENRY CECIL

BRIEF TALES FROM THE BENCH

What does it feel like to be a Judge? Read these stories and you can almost feel you are looking at proceedings from the lofty position of the Bench.

With a collection of eccentric and amusing characters, Henry Cecil brings to life the trials in a County Court and exposes the complex and often contradictory workings of the English legal system.

'Immensely readable. His stories rely above all on one quality – an extraordinary, an arresting, a really staggering ingenuity.'
New Statesman

BROTHERS IN LAW

Roger Thursby, aged twenty-four, is called to the bar. He is young, inexperienced and his love life is complicated. He blunders his way through a succession of comic adventures including his calamitous debut at the bar.

His career takes an upward turn when he is chosen to defend the caddish Alfred Green at the Old Bailey. In this first Roger Thursby novel Henry Cecil satirizes the legal profession with his usual wit and insight.

'Uproariously funny.' *The Times*

'Full of charm and humour. I think it is the best Henry Cecil yet.' P G Wodehouse

Henry Cecil

Hunt the Slipper

Harriet and Graham have been happily married for twenty years. One day Graham fails to return home and Harriet begins to realise she has been abandoned. This feeling is strengthened when she starts to receive monthly payments from an untraceable source. After five years on her own Harriet begins to see another man and divorces Graham on the grounds of his desertion. Then one evening Harriet returns home to find Graham sitting in a chair, casually reading a book. Her initial relief turns to anger and then to fear when she realises that if Graham's story is true, she may never trust his sanity again. This complex comedy thriller will grip your attention to the very last page.

Sober as a Judge

Roger Thursby, the hero of *Brothers in Law* and *Friends at Court*, continues his career as a High Court judge. He presides over a series of unusual cases, including a professional debtor and an action about a consignment of oranges which turned to juice before delivery. There is a delightful succession of eccentric witnesses as the reader views proceedings from the Bench.

'The author's gift for brilliant characterisation makes this a book that will delight lawyers and laymen as much as did its predecessors.' *The Daily Telegraph*

OTHER TITLES BY HENRY CECIL AVAILABLE DIRECT
FROM HOUSE OF STRATUS

Quantity		£	$(US)	$(CAN)	€
	ACCORDING TO THE EVIDENCE	6.99	11.50	15.99	11.50
	ALIBI FOR A JUDGE	6.99	11.50	15.99	11.50
	THE ASKING PRICE	6.99	11.50	15.99	11.50
	BRIEF TALES FROM THE BENCH	6.99	11.50	15.99	11.50
	BROTHERS IN LAW	6.99	11.50	15.99	11.50
	THE BUTTERCUP SPELL	6.99	11.50	15.99	11.50
	CROSS PURPOSES	6.99	11.50	15.99	11.50
	FATHERS IN LAW	6.99	11.50	15.99	11.50
	FRIENDS AT COURT	6.99	11.50	15.99	11.50
	FULL CIRCLE	6.99	11.50	15.99	11.50
	HUNT THE SLIPPER	6.99	11.50	15.99	11.50
	INDEPENDENT WITNESS	6.99	11.50	15.99	11.50
	MUCH IN EVIDENCE	6.99	11.50	15.99	11.50

ALL HOUSE OF STRATUS BOOKS ARE AVAILABLE FROM GOOD BOOKSHOPS OR
DIRECT FROM THE PUBLISHER:

Internet: **www.houseofstratus.com** including author interviews, reviews, features.

Email: **sales@houseofstratus.com** please quote author, title and credit card details.

OTHER TITLES BY HENRY CECIL AVAILABLE DIRECT
FROM HOUSE OF STRATUS

Quantity		£	$(US)	$(CAN)	€
	Natural Causes	6.99	11.50	15.99	11.50
	No Bail for the Judge	6.99	11.50	15.99	11.50
	No Fear or Favour	6.99	11.50	15.99	11.50
	The Painswick Line	6.99	11.50	15.99	11.50
	Portrait of a Judge	6.99	11.50	15.99	11.50
	Settled Out of Court	6.99	11.50	15.99	11.50
	Sober as a Judge	6.99	11.50	15.99	11.50
	Tell you What I'll do	6.99	11.50	15.99	11.50
	Truth With Her Boots On	6.99	11.50	15.99	11.50
	Unlawful Occasions	6.99	11.50	15.99	11.50
	The Wanted Man	6.99	11.50	15.99	11.50
	Ways and Means	6.99	11.50	15.99	11.50
	A Woman Named Anne	6.99	11.50	15.99	11.50

ALL HOUSE OF STRATUS BOOKS ARE AVAILABLE FROM GOOD BOOKSHOPS OR
DIRECT FROM THE PUBLISHER:

Hotline: UK ONLY: **0800 169 1780**, please quote author, title and credit card
details.
INTERNATIONAL: **+44 (0) 20 7494 6400**, please quote author, title,
and credit card details.

Send to: **House of Stratus**
24c Old Burlington Street
London
W1X 1RL
UK

Please allow following carriage costs per ORDER
(For goods up to free carriage limits shown)

	£(Sterling)	$(US)	$(CAN)	€(Euros)
UK	1.95	3.20	4.29	3.00
Europe	2.95	4.99	6.49	5.00
North America	2.95	4.99	6.49	5.00
Rest of World	2.95	5.99	7.75	6.00
Free carriage for goods value over:	50	75	100	75

PLEASE SEND CHEQUE, POSTAL ORDER (STERLING ONLY), EUROCHEQUE, OR
INTERNATIONAL MONEY ORDER (PLEASE CIRCLE METHOD OF PAYMENT YOU WISH TO USE)
MAKE PAYABLE TO: STRATUS HOLDINGS plc

Order total including postage:————Please tick currency you wish to use and
add total amount of order:

☐ £ (Sterling)   ☐ $ (US)   ☐ $ (CAN)   ☐ € (EUROS)

VISA, MASTERCARD, SWITCH, AMEX, SOLO, JCB:

☐☐☐☐☐☐☐☐☐☐☐☐☐☐☐☐☐☐☐☐☐☐☐

Issue number (Switch only):

☐☐☐

Start Date: Expiry Date:

☐☐/☐☐   ☐☐/☐☐

Signature: _____

NAME: _____

ADDRESS: _____

_____

POSTCODE: _____

Please allow 28 days for delivery.

Prices subject to change without notice.
Please tick box if you do not wish to receive any additional information. ☐

House of Stratus publishes many other titles in this genre; please
check our website (**www.houseofstratus.com**) for more details